BIG TIME

BIG TIME

Cynthia D. Grant

Atheneum New York
1982

LIBRARY OF CONGRESS CATALOGING IN PUBLICATION DATA

Grant, Cynthia D.   Big time.

SUMMARY: While waiting in Hollywood for a talent scout to make her little sister a star, Dory learns more than she wants to about the peculiarities of movie life.
    [1. Actors and actresses—Fiction] I. Title.
PZ7.G76672BI   [Fic]   81-8075
ISBN 0-689-30879-5   AACR2

Copyright © 1982 by Cynthia D. Grant
All rights reserved
Published simultaneously in Canada by
McClelland & Stewart, Ltd.
Composition by
American–Stratford Graphic Services, Inc.,
Brattleboro, Vermont
Printed and bound by Fairfield Graphics,
Fairfield, Pennsylvania
Designed by Mary M. Ahern
First Edition

*For Daniel,
Morgan, Dad, Mom, Chris, Peter and Rhonda;
the little people who help make it
impossible.
And for Dorothy and Linda
and especially,
for Michelle.*

BIG TIME

*L*ife is what happens to us while
we're making other plans.

Thomas La Mance

[I]

Something's wrong with my little sister, Missy, but try telling that to my parents. Missy craps ice cream, as far as they're concerned. She's the candy-apple of their eye.

I'm sick of her baby beauty pageants. I'm sick of her spangled boots. My big brother Bobby and I—we could light ourselves on fire in the living room and no one would notice. Not till intermission, and it never comes. Missy just goes on and on—she's always been like this, but she's getting worse. She says she'll be bigger than Shirley Temple and Judy Garland rolled into one. And in the front row egging her on—my parents.

Guess who gets the biggest bedroom, even though I'm seven years older? And a fancy mirror ringed with bulbs, so she can see herself in daylight, neonlight, starlight? Why isn't she riding a bike? Why can't she ever act normal? My friends have kid sisters; they giggle, they skin their knees. Not Missy. She plans everything she says and does, like a magician.

You should see her with grown-ups. It's sickening.

She has them eating out of her hand. Running their calloused fingers through her permed blonde curls. Her
eyes are so clear and blue you could drown in them, and
blank as a baby's if nobody's looking. But someone's
always looking, that's the thing with Missy. She's so
successful at nine, it's scary to think what she'll be like
by my age.

I don't know. Maybe I'm overreacting. But when
she talks to me, it's not like we're sisters. I could be anyone; I could be her secretary.

"Dory, would you get the phone? It's probably
for me."

Or: "Dory, if Mary Ellen comes by, tell her I'm
not home."

Once she said, "Dory, what's it like being plain?
Do you think it feels different than being beautiful?"

I was stunned. Not because she called me plain—
that's no news—but because it didn't occur to her she
was being cruel. It didn't even occur.

I don't know why it bugs me so much lately.
Mostly it's my parents. They don't seem to know what
to do with me and Bobby now that we're not little and
cute. We talk—he looks tough, but he's a real good guy,
and he's had it. He's fed up to here. He finished high
school last month so he works full time at the cycle
shop now, and on his own bike. That's all he ever does.
Soon as he gets enough money saved, he's gone. Somewhere, anywhere but Deadwood, Oklahoma. We're losing him, and Mama and Daddy don't even know. Like
the other night: he's telling them about his raise, then

Missy comes prancing and prattling in and spoils it, and he realizes they aren't listening and just stops—and nobody notices, only me.

It wasn't always this way. There's pictures of me and Bob in the albums; us and Santa, us at the fair. We had fun, I think. Missy has shelves of albums, reels of home movies. Tons of trophies. I mean tons. They cover the mantle over the pretend fireplace in the living room. Harvest Fair Princess, Sidewalk Sale Sweetheart, Top Twirler in the Tiny-Tot Division. School? The only thing she's interested in reading is a studio contract. She's going to be a superstar. I wonder. I mean, maybe she *will* take over the world, but what if she doesn't? What then?

Sometimes I picture Martians trying to pigeonhole people by studying my family. YOUNG MALES ARE MUTE, WEAR TORN LEVI JACKETS, AND CONTINUALLY TEAR APART AND REASSEMBLE FEROCIOUS TWO-WHEELED VEHICLES. YOUNG FEMALES EAT. AND WORRY AND EAT. WHEN NOT EATING, THEY WORRY ABOUT EATING. THEIR PARENTS, A MIDDLE-AGED COUPLE OF INDETERMINATE INTELLIGENCE, ARE TOTALLY ENGROSSED IN THE CARE AND FEEDING OF A CREATURE DIFFERENT FROM ANY PREVIOUSLY OBSERVED. SHE SINGS, SHE TAPS, SHE DRIVES ME BATS. She *practices* being spontaneous.

Life should be more like TV. When people cry on TV, they still look beautiful; but in real life they're ugly and red. At our house the TVs' always on, babbling in the background like some crazy old uncle. Dinnertime: Bobby gritting his teeth, Missy preening and prattling.

Mama and Daddy grinning, saying, "You can be anything you want, Baby. Sing that song Daddy likes . . ." Accompanied by a hysterical laugh-track.

Why can't we be a real family? Why is it so hard? I wish me and Bobby had a house in the country; an old house on a hill overlooking a highway going noplace special. Just going. He'd like that. I could write my poetry and he could work on his cycles, and we'd grow apples and carrots and cukes and chickens—not for killing, just for eggs. There'd be a pond out front floating two smug ducks, and flower beds and winding scarlet vines, and a wide front porch, and a real fireplace, and a grandfather clock nodding the days away. Evenings, we'd sit and watch TV; and Missy would be on every channel, singing, dancing, interviewing herself . . .

I talk about this with Byron. He's the one person, besides me and Bobby, who doesn't buy what Missy peddles. He's seventeen. My best friend. I met him when Bobby was beating him up once. Bobby's a lot different now. Byron's just the same.

He wears sandals and Hawaiian shirts and a wide-brimmed gray felt hat. His blond hair's a little too long. At school they used to call him "The Clam." That was during his silent period. Then he was all the time doing impressions. He did everyone but himself. You'd ask him a question and never know who'd answer; W. C. Fields or Marjorie Main.

He's fine now. He's Byron, but he does the voices, too. He's good with animals and plans to be a vet. He believes in reincarnation, says that's why we're not at home in Oklahoma. The other night he dreamed it was the 1930s and we were dancing in a European nightclub. We were elegant, we were artists, we were married. I wish I could've dreamed it, too.

There's no sex. That's not how it is with us. Daddy says it's not normal. What's normal? I'd go crazy if it weren't for Byron. I tell him everything. I tell him my parents seem like people in a play; that sometimes I believe I could walk out the door and never see them again and it would be okay. I tell him Bobby gets quieter and quieter. He used to be so funny and full of stories. I tell him my sister mushrooms like The Blob, consuming everything in her path. I tell him we move through the house like zombies, like strangers in a bus station, all waiting to go someplace else.

I tell him all this; he never interrupts, his eyes never leave my face. It's sunset; the sky's gone pumpkin as we sit on the front steps. Inside, Missy tortures her accordion. Bobby's engine screams. Byron gently tugs my braids and says, "That's showbiz, kid."

[2]

Missy's got her picture in the paper again. She's on the front page more often than the mayor. Deadwood's a small town; four thousand people. It doesn't take much to make news.

The picture, captioned "Plunge Into Summer!" shows this cute little girl (played by Missy) jumping off the high dive into the public pool. She's caught mid-air; a childlike smile lighting her face, her blonde hair looking like a shampoo commercial.

Of course, it doesn't show her landing just right, so her hair doesn't get wet, nothing short of a miracle. And paddling out just as quick as she can, so she doesn't get cooties. Missy's not too crazy about the public. She wants them to adore her and everything, but she doesn't want them touching her. She has this thing about germs. She's always washing her hair or taking a bath or something.

It goes on to say, blahblahblah, ". . . Missy, the daughter of Weyland and Lorraine Woods (formerly

Lorraine Jones, of Nowater), plans to enter the entertainment industry in Hollywood, as soon as possible."

I forgot: Missy's changing her name. She's to be known as Desiree Jones. We keep forgetting and calling her Missy. Byron calls her Attila.

I don't know what she's thinking; what kind of image she's trying to project. On the one hand, she wants to be Shirley Temple, and on the other, she's telling the newspaper reporter, "Come up and see me sometime!" in this weird Mae West impersonation. Mama and Daddy eat it up. She's just as cute as a bug! I know; she's my sister, I'm trying to love her. I do—but she sure makes it hard.

Everyone made a big fuss about it. "Saw your sister in the paper. She sure is cute!" She's not even cute; she's beautiful. I hate to say it, but it's true. She's so pretty I wish she were real, but she's not. She's Missy, and it's *not her fault*. The fault lies with two people who shall remain nameless. My parents. How can I love and hate them so much? Why won't they pay attention to me?

Last night me and Byron drove to Morgantown and went to a teen disco. It was the pits. Everyone wearing their teenager costumes and dancing all alike. The songs sounded the same, not a beat between them, played by some famous disc jockey I never heard of.

We danced; Byron's good. That always kind of surprises me. He's so tall he curves over a little, like a blond question mark.

We ran into some people from school wearing shiny vinyl clothes with glittery price tags hanging off them. They talked Big Bucks. Raymond Dickey said, "A car ain't a car unless it's a Porsche." "I guess none of us came in cars," Byron said, and the conversation dried up.

Back in Deadwood we parked on a little hill in the middle of nowhere and talked. If we went to my house, my parents would zoom in. When Missy's asleep, they find me fascinating.

My father's an electrician. I mean down to his bones. Our house is a science display. Supermarket doors with electric eyes. A burglar alarm that puts Fort Knox to shame. An intercom system so sensitive it can detect a sigh from any spot in any room. Weird, not to mention wired. I don't feel at home at home.

And if we go to Byron's, his dad comes out and acts pleased but as if he can't quite place us. Mr. Spears is the City Attorney. He's handsome, very silvery. He thinks Byron's the result of a hospital mix-up; someone got his kid, he got theirs. In the meantime he's grown quite fond of Byron, in a silvery kind of way. Mrs. Spears is an invalid. Has been for years. Having Byron took it out of her. She's a very pretty lady, but she's always in her room. Byron tries not to disturb her.

There they are in that big white house; the Mercedes in the driveway, Byron's old pickup parked out back. Mr. Spears is never sure whether we're adults yet or not, so he asks these awkward questions: How do we feel about marijuana? What's our opinion on the draft? When we tell him, he gets this look on his face like he wished he hadn't asked. But he asks. Daddy never asks me a thing. Typical conversation:

DADDY: How you doin', hon?
ME: Fine.
DADDY: School okay?
ME: Fine, Daddy.
DADDY: Good. Pass the squash.

I've considered telling him what I really think. "You want to know how I am? Lousy. I eat too much. I'm nervous all the time. I want everyone to be happy. Is that so much to ask? Missy's like a kite; she's so far out and nobody reels her in. I want to throw all her fake trophies in the fake fireplace and burn them. I want to love her but I don't have the strength."

I don't say that, of course. I say, "Fine, Daddy. Fine . . ." Who knows why; there's nothing to lose.

Mama said, "Have a good time at the disco last night?"

"Yes, Mama."

"Roger Hill called."

"Again?"

"I think you should go out with him, Dory. He's a very nice young man."

"Oh, Mama."

"You're seeing too much of Byron. You know I'm very fond of him, but he's not exactly, how should I put it—"

"He's my best friend."

"He's a boy, Dory."

"Yes, I know."

Mama married young. She was nineteen when she had me. She's a handsome woman, slender and soft, her brown hair piled up like a natural crown. And those blue Missy eyes. Mine and Bobby's are brown.

"You'll be graduating next spring. It's time you were getting serious."

"About what?"

"About what you plan to do. Whether you're going to go to college or get married."

"I'm never getting married, Mama. I don't want to be in parentheses."

"What's that mean?"

"In the wedding announcements. The bride's name's always in brackets."

"Oh, Dory. Don't tell me you're one of those women's libbers."

"All right, I won't."

No one in this family understands me.

Except Bobby. We went for a ride the other day. The road ribboned over the hills. There aren't many hills around here, so when you find some, you cherish them.

He was going too fast. I made him slow down. The clouds galloped overhead. I yelled over the cycle: "It's beautiful, Bobby!"

"What?"

"The view!"

"Yeah, nice!"

We got home after dark. Mama and Daddy met us at the door.

"Where were you? We were frantic."

"Bobby took me for a ride."

"You missed Missy's recital," Daddy said. "She was very disappointed."

"We went to one last week," I said.

"That was tap." Missy sniffed. "This was jazz."

"Sorry. We forgot."

Bobby didn't say anything.

Daddy said, "You think it's safe driving your sister around this time of night?"

"I can take care of myself," Bobby said.

"We're talking about your sister."

"Leave me out of this!" I cried. "I don't know *what* we're talking about!"

"What are you talking about, Dory?" asked Mama.

"I don't know! I can't put it into words! But everybody acts so crazy! Like we don't care about each other. We're supposed to be a family!"

"Oh, brother," Missy said. "Here we go again."

But I couldn't stop. The hurt gushed out.

"We've got to do something! I can't stand it anymore! Missy acting like a—"

"What? Like a what?" She's on her feet.

"Like a nut! So you want to be in show business! You're just a little kid. You don't know what's right!"

"And you do!"

"That's enough, Dory!" Daddy said.

"Leave her alone!" Bobby shouted. "She's right."

I was crying. I couldn't help it. You'd think I'd be used to this by now. It could be worse; I know our parents love us. They're just lost in this dream about Missy being immortal, or making commercials or something.

"There's something wrong with Missy! With all of us! We have to see a counselor!"

"A what?"

"A counselor! Someone who can tell us what's wrong!"

"You mean a psychiatrist?" Daddy said the word like "communist." "You think we should see a psychiatrist?"

"Yes!" I couldn't believe what I was saying.

"Nothing's wrong, Dory. You're overreacting."

"No, she's not, Mama." Bobby again.

"You agree with her?" Daddy's no villain. He does the best he can. He's always working, so we can have this nice house; so we can have everything a family should have, except each other.

"Yes, I do."

"I don't believe this!" Missy shrieked. "Just because Dory's jealous of me—"

"Jealous!"

"Well, you know you are!"

"Missy, sometimes—"

"Desiree," she said coldly.

Bobby laughed.

"At least I know where I'm going! Not like *some* people, who almost flunked out of high school!"

"You little brat!" Bobby grabbed at her.

[14]

"*Stop it! Stop it!*" I watched myself go crazy; screaming: "Stop it! Everybody stop!" till Mama got scared and shook me hard.

"Enough. That goes for you too, Missy. If Dory has a problem—"

"If *I* have a problem!"

"You've made your point, young lady. I'll make an appointment with the psychiatrist. We'll all go. You too, Bobby?"

"Wouldn't miss it."

"Now let's all sit down and have some Jello cake."

Missy kept saying she couldn't believe it. Daddy glared around the table then attacked and overpowered his dessert. I'm not trying to make trouble; I'm just trying to get things straight. We're drifting further and further apart. I'm afraid we'll get lost.

[3]

Right after Sunday dinner, following church, this guy shows up at the house.

There's a knock at the door, then the burglar alarm goes off like the world is ending. Daddy jumps up, barking, "Who's there?", peering through the built-in fisheye lens guaranteed to make Santa Claus look sinister.

This voice says, "I beg your pardon, but is this the home of Missy Woods?"

Everyone's ears prick up. "Who wants to know?"

"The name is Banks, sir. Robert Banks. I'm a Hollywood talent scout."

The alarm stops. The door opens. Mr. Banks steps in. He's tall and handsome, dressed all in white, with a wide-brimmed hat on his dark hair. Bobby puts down his cycle magazine and stares. We don't get many like Mr. Banks in Deadwood.

Daddy's saying, "Sorry about that. Short circuit in the wiring."

Mama manages to clear the table and produce tinkling glasses of iced tea in fifteen seconds.

We have lost Missy. At the words "Hollywood talent scout" she's gone into another dimension; into heights never before attempted without oxygen. She's Temple with just a *hint* of Garland.

"Come in, Mr. Banks. I'm pleased to meet you. I'd like to introduce my family. This is my mommy and daddy, and that's my brother and sister."

Bobby snickers, covering it with a cough.

"Pleased to meet you." Mr. Banks smiles, dazzling us with his teeth. How old is he? Thirty? Daddy looks so small beside him. I never realized how old he's getting.

"Weyland Woods, Mr. Banks. My wife, Lorraine. Son Bobby, and that's Dory."

"Bobby's name is Robert," Mama says, "but we always call him Bobby."

Everyone laughs. Mr. Banks sits in Daddy's leather chair.

"My friends call me Rob," he says. "Or Robert, either's fine."

"Care for some iced tea, Mr.—Robert?"

"No thank you, Lorraine."

"Could I get you something else? Coffee? A soda?"

"A Pepsi would be nice if you have one."

"Yes, I believe we do."

Mama sends a mental telegram to Bobby, who rolls his eyes and disappears. His Harley roars inconspicuously down the driveway. Minutes later he's back with the Pepsi. Mr. Banks takes it from the bottle.

Missy's going crazy. Her smile's eating her face. She's quivering with the strain of not screaming: "Will everyone shut up so he can talk?" She sits on the floor by Robert's feet, which are encased in leather boots. But not the kind everybody around here wears. They're soft-looking, fawn-colored, with smooth, high heels.

"Well, I suppose you're all wondering why I'm here," he says, and the small talk stops mid-sentence. "As I said, I'm a Hollywood talent scout, and I happened to see Missy's picture in the paper the other night, and I said to myself, 'Robert, there she is.' "

He smiles at Missy. Mama and Daddy smile at Missy. What's a Hollywood talent scout doing in Deadwood? People don't come here unless they have to.

"Lorraine, Weyland, I'll give it to you straight: I think your little girl has what it takes to make it big."

(*Missy's swelling, filling the room. We'll all be squashed!*)

"Of course, I've never seen her perform, but from what I hear, she's a very talented young lady."

"True," Daddy agrees. "Just what do you propose, Mr.—Robert?"

He spreads his slender fingers, netting everyone in the room.

"I'd like to represent your daughter. Be her manager. I know some people on the Coast—"

I'm inside Missy. I see what she's seeing. Palm trees, oranges, Disneyland. And beyond that, crowds; thousands of suntanned strangers, roaring like the surf: *Desiree, Desiree, Desiree . . .*

Everyone's gone into a trance. Mama comes out of it first.

"Missy's planned on a career in show business, Robert, but this is all so sudden."

"Mo-ther!" Missy wails.

"I know what you mean, Lorraine." Robert nods his handsome head. "But when opportunity knocks, we have to open the door."

I've heard that before. Bobby's graduation exercises. Something about detours on the path of life . . .

"Mommy! Daddy!" Missy jumps up and down. "Can you believe this? It's like a dream come true!"

"Hold on, young lady," Daddy says. "This is going too fast for me. You know how it is, Rob. You have children of your own?"

"I wish I did, sir." Robert could be an actor. He's too handsome to be real. If my best girlfriend Laurie saw him, she'd faint. He could say *ciao* and get away with it.

"Missy's our baby, Rob. We don't want nothing happening to her."

Including growing up. They'll never let her.

"I'm sure Robert understands," Mama says. "Couldn't you just show your friends pictures of her? We have movies, too; sound and everything."

"It wouldn't be the same!" Missy protests.

"I'm afraid your daughter's right, Lorraine. They'd need to see her in person to get the full impact."

Bobby kind of groans.

"Then you think we should go to Hollywood?"

"As soon as possible." Missy heads for the door. "Not right now, honey!" he says, and everyone laughs. She starts to pout, then thinks better of it.

"We'll need to discuss this, of course," Daddy says.

"Of course." Robert stands, shaking out the wrinkles in his cool white suit. He extends his hand; Daddy shakes it, Mama shakes it, Bobby takes it; he has no choice.

"Nice to meet you, Doris."

How did he know my name? Couldn't it have been Dorothea? Something fancy? Mr. Banks has come for Missy, not for me.

"If you want, I can do some of my routines," Missy says. "I sing and tap and play the accordion—"

"There'll be plenty of time for that," Robert promises.

We see him to the door, pressing forward for a look at his chariot, which turns out to be an old Ford station wagon, black and dusty, with California plates. It's not his real car; he's doing a friend a favor, driving it out to the Coast. The Ford doesn't look as if it will make it to the corner, but it starts right up, unwilling to disappoint him.

"I'll be in touch!" He waves and drives off.

"Weird," Bobby mutters. Missy explodes.

"Just because you're going nowhere fast doesn't mean you have to make fun of everything good that happens to me!" The strain of smiling for an hour overtakes her. Instant hysteria.

"What did I say?"

Daddy shoots Bobby a look and carries Missy inside, where she is quickly revived by the news that we're eating supper out, to celebrate.

"Celebrate what?" I ask. "Nothing's settled."

But I'm wrong.

In the course of my life I've ridden millions of miles in the Buick with my family. The Buick's different every year, but the ride's the same. Me and Bobby hunkered in back, Missy up front like a pet poodle, singing with the radio songs she knows. She knows them all.

All the way to the psychiatrist's she serenades us, interspersing the comment that it's "crazy for us all to go, since it's Dory's problem!" Sometimes refraining from socking Missy is like not scratching an itch.

Daddy grumbles, "I don't see why we just can't talk to Reverend Roy." He's our pastor at The Church of the True Believer.

"Because he's an ignoramus," Bobby says. Mama and Daddy expect lightning bolts to rain on the car. They don't go to church themselves; me and Missy are supposed to put in a good word for them with the Lord. Bobby quit going last year; flat refused. I hate it, but it's easier than arguing. And sometimes the hymns are nice, though usually the Reverend picks funeral music, which makes me think of worms and veins and death—not resurrection.

I don't like Reverend Roy. He sounds like he's on fire. He goes on about rock music and women wearing slacks, while the world goes to Hades in a hat. He sees everything in black and white, mostly white. Blacks can't join our church, though no one says so. There's so many things no one says but everyone knows.

Mostly I hate the way he does his boys. Ezekiel is Bobby's age and wild as the wind. He ran off last month, no one knows where. Jeremiah's my age, and nice as they come, but his dad treats him like a criminal. He's curfewed, grounded, and generally hounded. Once he and I and Byron picnicked by the river. Suddenly, the Reverend walks out of the bushes: "Jeremiah, go home and mow the lawn!" He pops up in the most unlikely spots: "Jeremiah, go clean the garage!" He's driving that boy crazy.

I am a True Believer. I believe in Jesus Christ. But I don't go around putting bumper stickers on my bicycle ("Jesus is Coming and He's Plenty Mad!") or carving a notch in my cross for converts. Everybody has to save themselves.

We get to Morgantown and drive to the psychiatrist's office, in a big new medical complex air-conditioned to the point of frostbite. In the waiting room we give our name to a receptionist with cool, bored eyes. Mama fills out a family history. Daddy reads *Field & Stream*. Missy reminds us, for the umpteenth time, that she's missing her accordion lesson.

I hope this guy knows what he's doing. Mama got his name out of the phone book. Byron said try to relax and enjoy it. His daddy sent him to one for years, until they figured out his only problem was being Byron.

The doctor's door opens; a couple comes out, crying and wiping their eyes. "He'll be right with you," the receptionist says, cutting off our escape.

We go in. The room's like stainless steel. Two full ferns hang in the window. The psychiatrist is young; he wears a vest and tie. He motions us to a cluster of incredibly uncomfortable chairs. I wonder if they're that way on purpose, or if he's never sat on our side of the desk. He produces a decorator box of Kleenex.

"Okay," he says. "What's the problem?"

Everyone laughs. Where do we begin? There's so much to say, I say nothing.

"First, let me get your names straight: Lorraine, Weyland, Missy, Bobby, Dory, right? I'm Doctor Bridges."

Byron called his shrink by his first name, which was Warren. They played Risk. Byron always beat him.

Silence falls across us like a shadow. Dr. Bridges taps a pencil on his desk. "I assume you're not paying fifty dollars an hour for the pleasure of my company," he finally says.

Daddy's moved to speak. "Frankly, Doctor, I don't know why we're here. I've never been to a psychiatrist before. Neither has my wife. My daughter thinks—"

"Which daughter?"

"Dory."

Dr. Bridges makes a note on his pad.

"She got real upset the other night and said we had to come here, so we did. That's all I know."

"Why were you so upset, Dory?" The doctor looks at me through a microscope; I'm some fascinating, mutated amoeba. My mouth's so dry. Everyone's staring.

"It's kind of hard to explain."

"Are you upset now?"

I'm too scared to lie. "Yes."

"Why?"

"Everyone's mad at me."

"Oh, Dory!" Missy's disgusted. It kills her to share the spotlight.

"Why do you think everyone's mad at you? Did they say so?"

"No . . . But they didn't want to come here."

"And you did."

"Not exactly."

"I see." He makes another note on his pad. "Why were you so upset the other night?"

Bobby's knee reassuringly presses mine. "Because everyone was acting so crazy."

"How?"

"Yelling and screaming—"

"You were the only one screaming," Missy says.

I try again. It's now or never. "My sister—"

"Sure! It's all *my* fault!" The veins stand out in her Barbie Doll neck.

"Missy, will you shut up so I can talk?"

"And let you make up a bunch of lies!"

[25]

"I'm not making up anything! It isn't normal, the way you act. Most little kids—"

"I'm not a little kid!"

"You can say that again."

"Stay out of this, Bobby," Daddy says.

"She keeps interrupting Dory!"

"Sure! Take *her* side! You've always hated me!" The tears erupt like Old Faithful.

"Why are you crying, Missy?" Dr. Bridges asks, offering the strategically-placed Kleenex.

"Because they hate me! You'd think they'd love me, but they don't! They're just jealous 'cause I get more attention than them!"

"She gets more attention than the Pope," Bobby says.

"Bobby, I'm warning you." Daddy again.

"If you don't mind, Mr. Woods," the doctor says. "Dory, do you love your little sister?"

"Yes." Missy looks surprised, Mama relieved. "But I don't like her. She's always showing off. We can't watch TV without her saying she could do it better. And her dance recitals!"

"What about them?" Missy's sobs almost drown him out.

"They're *endless!* And the beauty contests! She's nine years old! And everybody making such a big fuss about her—" I'm crying. Incoherent. I've failed.

Daddy takes over and explains that Missy tap-danced before she could walk. It's not that they push her; heavens, no. It's in her blood: she's a born star. And the other night Dory just blew up for no reason—

"She's always been high-strung," Mama adds.

Missy stops sniveling long enough to say, "Tell him about her poems."

Though at age four she did a bang-up version of "Twinkle, Twinkle, Little Star," Missy does not appreciate poetry. She regards it as just another of my afflictions; something scientists will someday cure.

"She's always writing these depressing poems," Missy says. "Like the one about clouds."

"What's wrong with clouds?"

"Nothing! It was the *way* you said it. Why do you have to be so serious? Can't you just enjoy life?"

I've given up reading my poems at the table. Bobby likes them, but he'd like anything I wrote. You'd think that would be enough, but it's not. I want to be really good at it. My parents think that's like being good at limping. They don't take me seriously. They take Missy seriously. That's how crazy they are.

"There's nothing wrong with Dory's poems!"

"Did you want to contribute something, Bobby?" Dr. Bridges asks.

"What's the use? They'll just twist it around. *They're* the ones with the problem, not Dory."

"You mean your parents."

"Yeah. And her."

"Your little sister? Why don't you use her name?"

"Her real name or her fake name?"

[27]

"It's not fake! It's for the stage!"

"*What* stage?"

"Bobby! Missy! Stop," Mama says.

"Well, why did we come here?" Bobby's yelling. "You don't listen, you don't let us talk. That little snot—"

"I'm not a snot! And what about Robert Banks? He thinks—"

Bobby ignores her. "—has you wrapped around her finger! You don't care about me and Dory. All you care about's her!"

"That's not true!" Daddy's furious. In the old days he would've thrown Bobby across the room. The last time he tried that, Bobby was fifteen.

"I'm sorry, Dory." Bobby's moving toward the door. "But it's too screwed up, and it's not gonna get any better."

"Not if you take that attitude," Mama says. "How are you going to get home?"

"Who cares?" The door slams behind him like a car crash.

After a pause Missy says, "He's been that way ever since he got his motorcycle."

Then they talk about Bobby's bike for a while, and how many friends he has, and if he ever gets in fights (only at home). And I see Mama and Daddy are baffled and hurt. They don't understand why we can't gladly serve Missy. They think slaves sing because they're happy.

I contemplate murder, mayhem, braticide. Again

and again I'm stabbing Missy; Orange Crush runs out. I think of things to say, but someone's always talking. Finally Dr. Bridges glances at his watch, flashes a digital smile and says, "Our hour's up."

We won't be back. It's hard for Daddy to take time off from work, and Mama drives Missy to her accordion lessons. Besides Missy's going to Hollywood. Dr. Bridges says I can come alone if I want to, but I'd have to borrow Byron's truck, and it seems like too much trouble.

I do not doubt, Lord, that the meek shall inherit the earth.

I'm just not sure we'll want it after the Missys get through with it.

[5]

It seems as if I notice being alive more than most people.

Sometimes I notice it so much I can scarcely breathe, never mind walk, talk or pass the rutabagas. I'm aware of being Here, Now: opening doors, brushing my hair, peering through holes in a fence.

Mama and Daddy have a knack for living that I never will. They're either in the past ("We should've —") or the future ("Next we'll—"), so they don't pay much attention to *now*, which is why it's always so slapdash and makedo.

THE TIME: The present. A Sunday afternoon.

THE SCENE: The home of Mr. and Mrs. Weyland Woods, Deadwood, Oklahoma, just prior to the arrival of Mr. Robert Banks, who will take us away from all this. He's bringing Missy's contract.

The Cast:

MR. AND MRS. WEYLAND WOODS. He, handsome at

forty-two in a worn, unlikely way. She, beautiful at thirty-six. Daddy thinks she's beautiful, too, but has never known how to tell her, probably never will.

THE SON: Exiting on motorcycle. I'm too close to know if he's handsome or not. To me, he's gorgeous; tries so hard and it never does any good. Drive carefully, Bob.

THE MIDDLE DAUGHTER: A shortish, tallish, fattish, thinnish, brown-haired girl near seventeen. Writes poetry when depressed, her normal state lately. Some of it good, some of it awful.

HER FRIEND BYRON: Tall and smiling. The scene passes before him like a parade.

And last but not least, the star of our show:

MISSY WOODS, also known as DESIREE JONES, aka THE FLAKE. Four foot two, eyes of blue, blonde hair, the works. Fully understands why John Cassavetes sold out Mia Farrow in *Rosemary's Baby*. Believes the shortest distance between two points is across someone's back. I have to remind myself it's *not her fault*. It would be so easy to blame, not to mention maim, her.

MAMA: I wonder what can be keeping Robert. He's fifteen minutes late.

DADDY: Probably the traffic.

MAMA: There's no traffic in Deadwood.

"Maybe his car broke down." I mean it sincerely, but Missy takes it as a crack and is properly miffed.

MAMA: His car didn't break down.

"Anyway, he'd call." My father.

BYRON: What time is it? Is Robert still coming?

And it starts again.

Missy looks like Tatum O'Neal done up as Dale Evans. She's quivering with excitement; her beaded fringe is flapping. If Robert doesn't get here soon, she'll explode and kill us all.

The TV's on, some show is blathering. Sports: the championship doughnut throws. Suddenly a car door slams. The set's off, and everyone's on. Daddy throws open the door.

"Come in, Robert! Come in, come in!"

A smile like the sun following an eclipse dawns on Missy's face, blinding me until I remember it takes more muscles to frown.

We're so glad to see him! Who wouldn't be? He's sky-dived in from a beer commercial; his navy blue jumpsuit unzipped to mid-chest, gold chains sparkling at his throat. If Missy were ten years older they'd be the perfect couple, on a soap. His name would be Jason, hers would be Heather. They'd have a beautiful but slightly defective baby named Cassie, whom doctors would be operating on *at this very moment!* Or maybe they'd be in real estate together.

Mama produces Pepsi from thin air, like a night-club magician.

"And this is Dory's friend Byron," Daddy's saying.

I can see from Byron's expression that Mr. Banks exceeds my description.

"His daddy's the city attorney," Mama adds, which is the nicest thing she can say about Byron.

"Pleased to meet you." Robert releases Byron's hand and wrings the Pepsi bottle dry. "My, but it's hot."

"Ninety-five in the shade," Daddy boasts.

Missy hasn't taken her eyes off Robert's briefcase. She believes it holds her future and can't wait to try it on. The adults touch briefly on world events. Missy disappears and returns with her batons. Byron's chin slides into his hand so only his pale moustache shows.

We're treated to a performance, complete with stereo marching music. When the applause dies down, Robert opens his briefcase. A hush falls over the crowd.

He produces the contract, a sheaf of typewritten pages. Mama speed-reads them. Daddy gets out his glasses.

"Everything seems to be in order." Mama sounds calm, but she's breathing like a bird. Her pretty print blouse rises and falls.

"It's standard," Robert says. "Ten percent's the going rate."

"Sounds fair to me." Daddy's pen won't work. As Robert hands him another, the sirens scream.

"What's that?" Robert's on his feet. "Another short circuit?"

"Afraid not." Daddy sprints around the room opening windows. "It's a twister."

"You mean a tornado?" Robert's pale beneath his tan.

"That's right." Mama expertly tosses china into the hall closet. "The sirens go off at City Hall."

Daddy opens the door. "Whoo! Look at that!" The

sky's green as an old bruise. Rain falls like lead. "Ever been in a tornado, Robert?"

"Can't say as I have."

"It's no big deal." Daddy rolls up rugs and stacks them in the corner.

"Dory, get the drinks." Mama dashes from the kitchen carrying a tray of clam dip and corn chips.

I grab the lemonade. Byron gets the glasses. Missy snatches the Pepsi out of the fridge. We hurry downstairs into the storm cellar, bolting the living room door behind us.

It's dark. Mama lights the lamps, illuminating rows of pickled cukes and beets, enough to live on for years. There's a radio and chairs, blankets and bottled water. Also a cot, which Missy commandeers, overcome by this ill-timed Act of God.

"Sorry for the inconvenience, Robert."

"It's not your fault, Weyland," Robert says graciously.

Daddy looks relieved. He turns on the radio. Nothing happens.

"Damn." He twists and turns the dials. He reaches for fresh batteries. "Where the— Dory, did you take those batteries?"

"No, sir."

"You sure?"

"Positive, Daddy."

"Then where are they?"

Missy knows I know. Otherwise she wouldn't speak.

"They're in my tape recorder, Daddy."

"In your what?"

"My tape recorder! I was listening to my voice."

"Jumpin' Judas, Missy—"

"Don't be mad, Daddy!"

"I'm not mad, honey. Shoot! Don't ever do that again."

"Care for some clam dip, Robert?" Mama asks. I pour the lemonade.

The wind shrieks, gasps, moans. I wonder where Bobby is. The strangest part about tornados is seeing what's left when they're gone.

"So this is your first tornado, Robert."

"Yes, ma'am. We don't get many in California."

"I imagine that's why property runs so high there. Of course, we don't have earthquakes here."

"They're a problem," Robert admits. "How long is this likely to last?"

"Not long." Mama produces the contract from her apron.

"Okay." Daddy raises his voice above the wind. "Let me get this straight. Just say Missy gets a million dollars per picture. You get a hundred thousand, right? What if she gets a percentage of the gross? I hear that's how they're doing it these days."

Robert pulls out a calculator. "Look here, Weyland." The twister hits, maybe a block away. The world is ending, the sky is falling. Jars of pickled beets crash, exploding like grenades. Somewhere an open door bangs, bangs, ba—

". . . of her percentage, see? So it always works out the same."

"I get it." Mama and Daddy are satisfied. Missy's blue eyes burn like gas flames.

"What do you think, hon?" Mama asks Daddy. It's staged; they've already decided.

"Looks good, hon, but what's important is what Missy thinks. We're talking about her future."

"Sign," Missy hisses, handing Mama a pen. She signs in that big, airy way. Daddy cramps in alongside her.

"When do we leave?" Missy cries. I've never seen her so happy. She even hugs Byron and me.

"Soon." Robert's gold chains glitter.

"Oh, I've got so much to do!" Mama says. "Packing and planning. Dory, you'll have to—"

"I'm going." Even the wind falls silent. "I'm going to California with you and Missy." I don't know where that came from. But as soon as I say it, I know it's true.

"You can't! Daddy and Bobby will be here alone!"

"They'll be fine," I say, though I doubt it.

"Why should you go?" Missy shrieks. "This has nothing to do with you!"

"It's my summer vacation, too! Why should I stay in Deadwood while you have all the fun?"

"It's not supposed to be fun! It's business!"

"Bull!"

"Doris!" Daddy starts, but I rise like the wind.

"I'm going! I don't care *what* you say! And Byron's going with me! And if you try to stop us, I'll kill myself, or run away, or go crazy!"

"She's already crazy," Missy says.

"Dory—"

"I mean it, Mama! I'm not staying in Deadwood. There's nothing to do here but sweat. I'm going to California with you, and Byron's coming with me!"

She tries to stare me down then looks away. "Doris has been under a strain lately," she tells Robert.

"There's plenty of room in the Ford," he says mildly.

"Byron, do your folks know about this?"

"Not yet, Mr. Woods, but I'm sure they'll be pleased. They've always wanted me to travel." If Byron said he was going to Mars, his dad would say, "Got enough money?"

"I suppose there's no reason why they can't go," Mama says.

"I suppose not," Daddy agrees reluctantly. "You could use another man along."

"What's that got to do with Byron?" Missy bleats.

"Then it's settled," Robert says pleasantly. "What day is this? Sunday? Can we be ready by Tuesday?"

Missy can be ready in fifteen minutes, but Mama says Tuesday's fine. Byron points out that the tornado's over. The all's-well sirens are screaming.

We climb the stairs. Daddy opens the door. Sunlight falls on our faces. The room's much the same as we left it, but drenched. Bobby's pushing waves around with a mop.

"We were worried, Bobby."

"I'm here, Mama."

"Guess what, Bob!" I can't help hugging him. "Me and Byron are going to California!"

He looks at me, then at Missy, and laughs. Mr. Banks declines further clam dip. We see him to his car, which is remarkably intact. The rest of the neighborhood has been destroyed.

"Thanks for coming by, Robert."

"My pleasure. See you Tuesday." He heaves a dead heifer off the hood and drives away.

I invite Byron for supper because the roof will cave in as soon as he's gone.

But I don't care. I'm going to California.

[6]

"Dory, did you pack your pink blouse?"

"I hate that blouse, Mama. It makes me look like a pig."

"Bring it, and bring the green dress, too."

"What for?" I've packed my jeans, my bathing suit, my suntan oil. That seems sufficient.

"Dory, I don't have time to argue." Mama's planned for this morning all her life, but she's still running behind schedule.

Missy pops in as Mama pops out. "Dory, can I use your razor?"

"Sure. Hold out your wrists."

"Very funny."

She examines her underarms in the mirror, runs her hands down her pale baby legs. She can't wait to shave. Who knows why. It just grows back. In seconds. My legs look ridiculous: bare shins and mohair thighs. Why stop at the knee? Why not shave my head?

I'm seriously considering not shaving at all. It seems

so pointless, doing it over and over. Mama says that's like saying why make the bed, you're just going to sleep in it again. Exactly.

"Did Mama say you could shave your legs?"

"I didn't have time to ask."

"Well, ask." I'm not having Mama mad at me just so Missy can feel mature. She flounces out.

Getting ready's the worst part of going somewhere. There's so much to remember. Mama's tacked a zillion lists all over the house: *Don't forget the zinnias. Casserole's in the freezer. Remember to bribe the paperboy* . . . It's unclear how long we'll be gone. A month at the outside, Mama says. Unless Missy becomes a megastar and takes the world by storm. I don't know what will happen then. Maybe Mr. Banks will adopt her. Maybe we'll adopt him.

I can't picture us moving to California. It's the kind of place you vacation; you win two weeks there in a cereal-box contest. It's always sounded like a dream state. It doesn't snow, except where it's supposed to. The heat's dry, not damp like here. The people are golden: suntanned and blond. There's movie stars, avocados, homosexuals and no winter. My girlfriends are dying of envy.

"Gol, you lucky dog!" Laurie said. She made me promise to photograph the ocean with my mind, so I could describe it down to the seashell. Laurie's never seen the ocean. Me neither, and I've missed it all my life.

"How you doin', hon?" Daddy sticks his head in.

As usual, he looks worried, like he's thinking of something else.

"Fine, Daddy." Until this moment I haven't realized how much I'll miss him. The strangest feeling grips my throat. I want to hug him and not let go. He doesn't want us to leave—especially them—but he'd never spoil Missy's big chance.

He looks at his watch. "Robert will be here soon."

"Daddy?"

"What, hon?"

"Nothing. I'll get ready."

When I'm home, I don't want to leave; when I leave, I don't want to go back. Why do I prize falling stars? The house looks so comfortable, cool and clean. Missy's trophies gleam on the mantle. My room may be small, but it's all mine, a tidy little island.

Byron arrives with a bashed-up suitcase. He and Missy start in. "Promise you'll forget me when you're famous," he begs. Bobby asks if I need any help.

"Thanks, Bob. Everything's under control."

"That's what *she* thinks," he tells Byron.

Mr. Banks toots his horn in the driveway. Mama goes into high gear.

Seeing Daddy carry all our stuff out to the car . . . "He'll be fine," Bobby says, reading my mind. We pack; there's a solid wall behind the back seat. Mostly Missy's stuff: her clothes, tap shoes, accordion.

Mama keeps running into the house, remembering one last thing. Daddy and Robert pore over maps.

"You sure you'll be all right?" Mama asks Daddy.

"We'll be fine, won't we, Bobby."

"Jimdandy."

"Are you okay?" Byron whispers. He doesn't miss a trick.

"I will be, soon as we get out of here." I hide behind my new mirror sunglasses.

"Are we ready?" Robert's a jovial cruise captain, in his perfectly faded jeans and white cap.

"Ready as we'll ever be," Mama says doubtfully.

Daddy scoops up Missy. "I'm going to miss my baby girl!"

"Oh, Daddy! I'm not a baby!" she gurgles, sliding out of his arms and into the front seat.

"Bye, darlin'." Mama and Daddy hug.

"You eat!" she says sternly. "And don't worry."

"I will," he says. "I mean I won't." Everyone laughs.

"Bye, Bobby." I bury my face in his neck. "Take care of yourself, hear?"

"You, too."

"I love you, Bobby."

"Me, too." He gently pushes me away.

Daddy hugs me and strokes my hair. "Bye, honey. Be a good girl."

"I will. Don't be lonely, Daddy."

"Lonely! You'll be back before you know it."

"Not if I'm famous!" Missy yells.

Bobby asks if we can get that in writing. Robert

shakes Daddy's hand. Me and Byron get in back, Mama up front, next to Missy.

"Okay, go down to the corner and make a left . . ."

Robert listens to Daddy's directions as if for the very first time. It's a gorgeous morning, the sun is shining, and I feel as if my life is ending.

"Dory?" Byron presses my hand. "We're going to California."

"I know. I don't know what's wrong with me." I quietly blow my nose.

"Missy will be famous, you'll marry a surfer—"

"I'm never getting married. Do you really think she'll be famous?"

He leans close, pressing his mouth to my ear, doing his W.C. Fields. "In my opinion, this guy's a flake. I think he's got the hots for your mother."

"Thanks again, Weyland. We'll be in touch!" Robert starts the car, and we rumble down the runway.

"Bye, honey! Bye, Bobby!"

"Call," Daddy says. "Drive careful."

We hang out the window, blowing kisses. Robert honks the horn. Daddy and Bobby get tiny behind us, waving till we turn the corner.

[7]

Dear Bobby,

Greetings from Slow Death, New Mexico; home of Fat Phil's 24 Hour Restaurant and Truckstop, where grease isn't a movie, it's a way of life.

I would've written sooner but the last few days have been crazy. Things went wrong the minute we left Deadwood.

We got two flat tires as we got on 66. Byron and I fixed them. Missy played her accordion. Then the horn got stuck outside Amarillo. It stopped after a while. Then the antenna snapped off, don't ask me how; this whole thing is like a disaster movie. Missy insisted we go back for it so she could have her music. I'd forgotten how awful she is on trips: "I'm too hot, cold, hungry, thirsty, wretched—" A real trouper.

Then Robert stopped for gas and forgot me and Byron. We were still in the bathrooms. We come out; the Ford's disappearing. Fortunately, Mama noticed we were missing. It's been weird.

We're eating corn dogs, burgers, take-out food. My stomach's a mess. We have to stop every few hours so Robert can stock up on Pepsi. It's a wonder there's a tooth in his head.

The first night we slept in a sleazy motel; me and Mama and Baby Jane in one room, Byron and Robert in the other. The next motel was better; no lipstick on the glass in the john, and a Continental breakfast too, made of genuine Continentals.

On Thursday, I guess it was Thursday, we made it to Last Ditch and had our picture taken in front of the hanging tree. It has a gold plaque and everything.

We've been taking zillions of pictures in case we want to remember this. Yesterday we stopped on a cliff, and Byron took the camera and said, "Everybody move to the right. No, the left. Now move back, Missy. Farther, farther . . ." Mama didn't think it was a bit funny, though Missy was nowhere near the edge

Last Ditch was awful strange. The clocks stopped in 1955. All the women had beehive hairdos and the men looked like Roy Rogers, even more than at home. We stopped at a Ribs 'N' Run for lunch, and it was incredible. The scene featured:

a) a drunk boy about fifteen with half his teeth missing trying to start a fight

b) a hippie of undetermined sex with rhinestone earrings trying to bum a burger
c) a Black boy of twelve or so, whom two fat, over-made-up, ultracheap girls called a nigger. He started crying. Then one of them tried to apologize: "I didn't mean that the way it sounded."

Then a bunch of cowboys came in and got rowdy, and the ribs started to fly. But you know Mama: we'd paid for our meal and we finished it.

Now we're at Fat Phil's while Mama and Robert try to get the carburetor fixed. The guy said he couldn't get the part till next week, and Robert got mad and said, "What're you going to do? Drive back to Detroit for it?" The car should be ready soon. I hope so. This place gives me the creeps. It's full of truckers and cowboys and CB radios and girly magazines. If Byron's not sitting right here, guys invite me outside to look at their rigs.

Something strange happened a while ago. As the waitress was dishing up our mushroom soup, she looked at Robert, smiled and said, "Reverend! Praise the Lord!" We figured she was some kind of nut, but Robert explained that at one time he *was* a man of the cloth, but gave it up because of some tragic and vague event we couldn't weasel out of him. Mama keeps wondering if he was ever married, but he's never said. Then Byron said he was a minister too, in the Church of the Total Transaction. He sent two dollars to a box number in Tulsa, and now he can perform weddings, funerals, seances, etc. Mama said that wasn't the same thing at all, even after he showed her his wallet-sized credential.

I just ate a gray chicken sandwich, Bobby. No kidding. It was gray.

Even as I write, another tragedy is unfolding. Mama and Robert have just come back and are breaking the horrible news that Robert has somehow lost all his money. The four thousand dollars he had in his wallet is gone.

"Just calm down, Missy" Mama's saying. "Cork it."

"But now we'll have to go home!" She buries her head in her arms, knocking her milkshake into Byron's lap.

Everyone in the place is staring. The waitress is coming back.

"Is everything okay, Reverend?"

"Fine. Just fine. Could we have another milkshake here? What flavor, Missy?"

"Strawberry," Byron says.

"Robert, I'm so sorry," Mama says. "Maybe you should call the sheriff."

"I will, but you know human nature. It'll be a miracle if the money turns up."

"Amen," Byron murmurs.

"Anyway, there's no need to worry. I have plenty of money, and my credit cards—"

"I couldn't, Lorraine. It wouldn't be right."

"You can pay us back after Missy starts working."

The tiny trouper lifts her tousled head. "Please, Robert? For me?"

Who could resist? He reconsiders. "We've come so far, it'd be a shame to turn back now."

"Hallelujah!"

"Byron, you're running that minister thing into the ground," Mama says. She's leaving to call Daddy to wire more money. Robert's gone to phone the sheriff. Missy's blowing bubbles in her milkshake. Don't you wish you were here?

I better go, Bob. Say hi to Daddy and tell him everything's fine. I'll let you know where we are as soon as we get there.

Your loving sister,
Dory

[8]

I used to picture Hell, as rendered by the Reverend Roy Tarbox, as rivers, valleys, fountains of flame in purple, puce, vermillion; the air rent with the smoky screams of nudes holding flashlights under their chins.

Not so. Hell is a black Ford station wagon in the middle of the desert in the middle of the summer, packed with four sweaty adult-types and a kid who won't stop singing. I've begged her. All we can get is a country-western station, and if I hear any more about broken marriages, I'll scream.

We've left 66; we're taking a shortcut through Las Vegas, which is like taking a shortcut through Hong Kong. Mama's pleased.

There's no scenery; just the hot blue sky and land as flat and brown as butcher paper. Byron and I haven't spoken since I asked him to knock off the Johnny Cash impression. Fortunately, Missy hasn't noticed.

"What's that?" She points ahead to the first landmark in miles: a hitchhiker, a man dressed in black, who doesn't get much taller as we get closer.

"Strange place to hitchhike," Mama says, "in the middle of the middle of nowhere."

"Yes." Robert steps on the gas. Just as we're about to blast past him, the hitchhiker pulls something green from his pocket and waves it in the air.

Robert stops on a dime. He leans across Missy and Mama and asks, "Where you going?"

"Nowhere fast." The hitchhiker tosses his suitcase in back and hops in between Byron and me. He's got curly dark hair, impenetrable sunglasses, and a trim black moustache and beard. Though he's dressed for winter in the turkey-killing heat, he doesn't seem to sweat.

"Nice of you to stop," he says. "Thought you could use this for gas."

"Thanks." Robert pockets the ten. "The name's Banks. My friends call me Rob. Or Robert, either's fine."

"O'Hara," the hitchhiker says with a smile. He shakes hands all around.

"You're a long way from home, Mr. O'Hara." Mama never asks direct questions; she sets little traps instead.

"Yes, ma'am. I was beginning to wonder if I'd ever get a ride. People don't stop like they used to."

"Too many nuts running around," Robert says. "Where you headed?"

"Vegas, till my car broke down."

"Where?" Byron asks. "We didn't see it."

"Cleveland."

O'Hara takes off his glasses. His eyes are black holes in space. He looks Robert's age, but it's hard to tell. Hair covers most of his face.

"What kind of work do you do, Mr. O'Hara?" Mama turns politely in her seat. Missy gives him the deep freeze. She thinks beards are un-American.

"I'm in sales, ma'am."

"Really? How interesting."

"Fascinating," Missy says.

He chain-smokes Lucky Strikes, lighting the next from the last. He drums his fingers, taps his toes, checks the rearview mirror.

"You folks on vacation?"

"Hardly," Missy says.

Robert explains who and what we are, which takes less time than you'd think. He and O'Hara have hit it right off. They seem to talk in code.

"Georgia," Robert sighs.

"Michigan!" O'Hara snickers. He's working his way cross-country, stopping in Vegas to pick up some change.

"I've got a system. Blackjack."

"Everybody's got a system," Robert says.

"But this one works."

"How much?"

"Ten."

"What do you take me for?" Robert laughs.

"Anything I can get."

Most of the time we don't understand; they speak

a foreign language. Still, the hours fly. O'Hara's full of stories. He's been a truck driver, sky diver, dance instructor, chef. Likes brandy, Cajun music, and chess, loves chess. Talks it up like some men talk up sex.

"It's life. It's the ultimate game. Whether you know it or not, everybody's trying to beat you."

"That's stupid." Missy turns up the radio.

"No it's not, little darlin'," he says the way he'd say "Shut yer mouth or else." "Darlin', would you mind turning down the volume? That horse music's giving me a headache."

"Tough toenails."

Mama leans over and turns it off. "I'm hungry!" Missy wails.

"We'll be in Poker Flats in a couple of minutes," Robert says. "We'll get something there."

A sheriff's car appears in the rearview mirror. O'Hara hits the floor. After it passes he sits up and says, "Rob, got a butt?"

"Don't smoke."

"Filthy habit," O'Hara agrees. "That's a nice place. I've been there." He points to a big brick restaurant called The Harbor. Mama says that sounds fine. Robert parks the car.

Byron carefully unpacks himself. Missy hops up and down; has to wee!

"Well, don't stand there like a ninny! Run inside!" Mama says. "Aren't you coming with us, Mr. O'Hara?"

"No thank you, ma'am. I'll join you later."

"Take care." Robert ushers us in.

It's dark and cool as the belly of a shell. We stumble past the bar into the dining room.

It's dinnertime and packed. The clatter of forks is overwhelming. Robert melts the hostess with a smile; we get a table and order drinks. Pepsi for Robert, an old-fashioned for Mama, and Shirley Temples for "the kids."

"Oh, it's so good to get out of the car!" Mama's combed her hair and freshened her lipstick. "Dory, will you take off those awful glasses? I'm sick of staring at myself."

Missy's the only one who doesn't mind them. She uses them to check her hair.

"How long before we get to Vegas?" Byron asks. We still aren't speaking.

"Not long," Robert says. "Two or three hours."

Mama just about swoons.

"To think I'm going to see Las Vegas! I wonder if Sammy Davis will be there. And Dean Martin! I just love the way he sings! He makes it sound so easy!"

"That's the truth," Byron says.

Suddenly Mama's overcome with guilt: she's having too much fun. She excuses herself and goes to phone Daddy. Robert hides behind his menu.

We make him nervous, Byron and I. Teenagers affect lots of people that way. Daddy, for instance, or Mr. Spears. They're afraid we'll want the truth, or tell it. Mama's more at ease but still not normal, even when it's just the two of us. She told me about my period, but she's never mentioned sex. I don't know when she's planning to get around to that.

The waitress arrives. Robert orders for Mama. She comes back to the table smiling.

"Daddy and Bobby send their love. The washing machine broke. Roger Hill called, Dory."

"So?"

"Sew buttons on an iron shirt!" Missy yelps. "When's the food gonna get here?"

I hate watching her eat. She shovels it in and never gains an ounce. The calories convert to sheer nerve. Also, she talks with her mouth full.

"You're not eating much, Dory." Robert's concerned.

"I guess I'm not too hungry."

"She thinks she's fat," Missy manages through mashed potatoes. "She's always trying to diet."

"You don't need to diet," Robert says.

"I'd like to lose ten pounds."

"Five off each hip. Just kidding!" Missy brays.

"You're a riot," Byron says, and we're talking.

"Mmmm, delicious dinner, Robert." Mama polishes off her prawns. "I wish Mr. O'Hara could've joined us."

"He has." I point my fork.

Dressed in a crisp tuxedo, he's going from table to table, murmuring, "How was your dinner? Is everything all right? Can I get you anything else?" He's also collecting the tip trays.

"Mr. O'Hara!" Mama touches her napkin to her lips. "I didn't know you worked here."

"Just picking up a little extra money. How was your dinner?"

"Wonderful!"

"Can I get you more coffee?"

"That'll do it," Robert says. "Meet you outside."

And we leave, abruptly, and get in the car. Robert starts the engine. In a minute O'Hara comes out in his civvies, jumps in, and we drive off.

"Nuts," Missy says. "I forgot to get a toothpick."

But we don't go back for one. We drive on, on into the night.

I begin to be grateful for Mr. O'Hara, because he makes me feel so normal by comparison. He's very intense. Sirens make him wince. Everything he says is crazy, but he *listens* when I talk, which is more than can be said for most people. He's twenty-five.

"Dory, Dory, Dory. I get the impression your name is . . . Dorothea! Am I right?"

"Wrong," Missy says. "It's Doris."

"Thanks, Missy."

"It's not *my* fault!"

"Doris is a perfectly good name," Mama says. It was Grandma's. She died five years ago, and I still miss her fierce.

O'Hara says, "I like Doris."

"You would," Missy sneers.

The miles fly. O'Hara talks and talks. An unending stream of tar and nicotine enters his chest, poisoning him; he talks about that and keeps doing it.

At one time he worked as a bouncer in a bar. He told everyone he knew karate. He has a tattoo on his arm he can't remember getting: MARGE, in a crimson heart. He plays the organ; in jazz bands, pizza pits, cathedrals. Missy pretends to snore.

The night is as eternal as the highway. A million stars, rings on black fingers, splash color; then suddenly fall from the sky to frame a city made of money, in the middle of the desert, like a mirage.

"It's just like I pictured it!" Mama cries.

The night's as bright as day. A zillion neon light bulbs chase each other up and down the street. The sidewalks pulse with people.

"Will you be in town long?" Robert asks O'Hara.

"Depends how my luck's running."

"Good luck," I say.

"You'll need it," Missy adds.

We've been so nice O'Hara wants to return the favor. He's just launching into the dollar ninety-eight version of "The System" when a car, a Caddy convertible with the top down, roars up alongside us. There's two giant guys in it, both pointing at O'Hara and start-to get awful mad.

"I'll lose them," Robert says.

"Thanks anyway, Rob. I'll get out here. Goodbye, everybody. Enjoy Las Vegas. Dorothea"— he kisses my hand—"take care."

And grabbing his suitcase, he opens the door and jumps out—we're doing thirty-five down the main drag. And the last we see of him, he's disappearing around a corner; in no real danger, except from himself.

[9]

We leave Missy, screaming, in the casino child-care center. The casino's called The Gold Rush. The Kiddy Korral's packed with kids. Some of the little ones are sleeping in a room lined with cots. The main room has couches and beanbag chairs and a giant color TV screen on one wall. A whole bunch of silent kids are staring at a shrieking comedy.

"How come Dory doesn't have to stay here? She always has all the fun!"

"Missy," Mama says. "You're acting like a little child."

"I *am* a little child."

"We'll bring you a nice present," Robert says. "What would you like?"

"Eternal life."

"Oh, drop dead, Byron!"

We escape, promising to bring her a pretty, and enter the gleaming stream feeding the casino.

Robert has changed his clothes (again) and women

turn to look. A few men, too. He's splendidly slim in Levi pants and a vest, soft sandals hugging his bare brown feet. His toenails are clean. One thing about Robert: he's just as good up close. There's no hair growing out of his nose. His breath's sweet as a baby's.

Mama's changed too, into her yellow dress. She looks like an ad for summer. Her sun-streaked hair is long and loose. She looks younger than me.

"Now remember," Robert tells me and Byron, "technically you're not supposed to be here. You're minors."

"We'll try not to act too childish," Byron promises.

"Don't play the machines, don't call attention to yourselves—"

Mama stops to take a picture. The camera isn't halfway to her eye before she's surrounded by gray security guards.

"Sorry, lady. No pictures in the casino."

"She didn't know," Robert apologizes, and the guards disperse like smoke.

Mama's pink with confusion and embarrassment.

"What's the matter, Robert? What did I do?"

He explains that some people might not want their pictures taken gambling, or someplace other than where they said they'd be, or with someone else's husband or wife.

"Of course." Mama pockets the Instamatic, and we enter the biggest room I've ever seen.

It's a city; the air's thick with cigarettes and the metallic voice of millions. People are feeding slot machines: dimes, quarters, dollars. Some people hold down several machines and snarl if you get too close. For those too exhausted to pull the handle, there're buttons you push with your nose. People are swiping dirty ashtrays. Guards wheel sacks of money by. Women with change belts take bills, return silver. Other women in tight satin shorts sell drinks, or even give them away, compliments of the management. Lights flash, bells ring—we're inside a giant pinball machine.

Robert and Mama leave to play cards. Blackjack's Robert's game. We agree to meet in two hours by the crap tables, though how we'll know when it's time, I don't know. There are no clocks, anywhere. Just like out at the new shopping mall in Elvira: they don't want you to go home and eat or sleep, they just want you to shop and shop. The only place you see clocks these days is outside funeral homes.

Mama and Robert disappear. Byron and I try to act inconspicuous. Which is fantastically easy, because no one's interested. We don't pay off.

Smoky music pours from the darkened lounge. Herds of people push past. Byron bumps into a guy playing a dime machine and almost gets eaten. Cleanup crews in olive drab sweep expertly, invisibly, around the players.

We watch the roulette wheel for a while, the little ball leaping and bouncing. Some of the gamblers are glamorous and beautiful, but there're others in stained polyester and pajamas; women in curlers and men with shaving nicks patched with pink toilet paper.

A middle-aged man is feeding Big Bertha, a silver dollar every bite. A crowd gathers, but he runs out of money and everyone drifts away. Except for one old lady who takes a dollar out of a sock in her purse, kisses it and puts it in. The machine lights up like Christmas morning. Bells ring! Hallelujah! Silver dollars are pouring out, and the man, who's been watching, goes crazy.

"That's my money! That's my machine! Don't touch that money! It's mine!"

The crowd reforms as the old lady stuffs silver dollars into her sock.

"That's *my* money! I was playing that machine! I've been playing it for hours!"

The security guards materialize and swarm all over the guy. A cashier gives the lady eight one-hundred-dollar bills, which she tucks in her sock, which she tucks in her purse. They're dragging the guy away . . .

A sign invites us to hear a talk about real estate in Florida. If we do, they'll give us fifteen dollars in scrip to play the machines, so we go.

A bunch of couples wait to get in, young and new-married looking. The doors open, and we crowd inside; but instead of getting to sit in the bleachers, we're herded to little round tables with a salesman at each one.

Our salesman, whose name is Dick, Doug, or Don, opens a bottle of champagne. He stands and introduces us to the crowd: "I'd like you to meet Mr. and Mrs. Lawrence Welk, from Deadwood, Oklahoma." Everyone claps. We clap for everyone else.

Then the lights go off, and we watch a movie featuring an actor who used to be famous. He warns us we can't afford to pass up the chance to be his next-door neighbor. We must buy a piece of Alluvial Terrace and build a model home on it. Only they don't show him from the waist down because he's up to his knees in swamp. Gator Acres, Byron whispers. Hot and cold running water moccasins.

Then the lights go on, and they wheel in a diorama of Alluvial Terrace made by a kindergarten craft class, with a big mirror behind it to round things out. They try to sell it to us.

Our salesman shuffles two stacks of blueprints; one for the houses, one for the lots. We explain we can't afford two hundred dollars a month, or fifty, or fifteen. He throws in the towel and finishes the champagne. He tells us how lousy his new car runs. We tell him about the Ford. Then his manager, a huge, handsome guy, comes by, finds out we're poor, curls his lip, throws the scrip at us, and we slink out.

And win two seven fifty jackpots. And blow it all on Keno tickets. And spend six dollars on two cheese sandwiches you'd expect to find in a joke shop. Then it's time to meet Mama and Robert.

They're not there. I picture them running down the street, hand in hand, stopping at a Divorce-While-U-Wait place. Then nipping next door to the Chapel of the Cheesecake and tying on the bonds of holy matrimony . . . Not likely. But who knows what Mama will do these days? She's a stranger, stranger every minute.

They arrive, flushed with triumph. Robert won thirteen hundred dollars. Mama flabbergastedly tells us about his system. He stops to buy Missy a tacky little purse with the words FABULOUS LAS VEGAS in neon sequins.

At the Kiddy Korral Missy's telling a little girl with long brown braids how she's going to be a star—make records, commercials, movies and a mint—and the little girl's drinking it in. She thinks Robert's our father and Mama's our mother and we're one big happy family. When we leave, she follows with her baby deer eyes, and I want to run back and slap her face, I want to hold her till she falls asleep.

[10]

I'm awake. *Where am I?* My heart feels squeezed. Then I remember: another motel.

Light filters through the venetian blinds and the TV's on—no, it's Mama, by the window, talking to a man with his face in shadow. Robert?

The door blows open and Missy sweeps in, in a huge, pink, southern belle dress. She's got a flamingo— no, a bonnet on her head.

"Doesn't she look lovely?" Mama says.

"Takes after her mother," the man murmurs.

I start to sit up but my nightgown's gone. I don't want the man to see my breasts.

"Missy," I say, "how come you're all dressed up?"

"*Miss* Missy to you." She fans herself.

Suddenly Byron's absence is a blaring horn. Something's Really Wrong.

"Where's Byron? Mama, what's happening?"

"Dory, I'm afraid we have bad news."

"Where is he?"

"Lost!" Missy says cheerfully. "And frankly, I don't give a damn!"

"Don't swear, darlin'," Mama says vaguely.

"Fiddle-dee-dee!" she replies.

There's a roaring in my head; a river rushes toward my eyes.

"How could you possibly lose Byron?"

"Wasn't easy," Missy admits. "We had to work at it."

Tears veil the room. Everything's wavy and underwater. Mama floats across the floor and settles on my bed. The man remains by the window.

"Dory, there's something else I have to tell you."

I know what it is. My heart stops.

"You're letting me go! Is that it, Mama? You're not renewing my contract!"

"What a ham," Missy says.

"It's nothing personal, Dory." Mama rises. The man opens the door.

"Don't go, Mama! I promise I'll be pretty!"

"Fat chance"—Missy snickers—"if you'll pardon the pun." She scoops up her skirts and taps out.

Mama floats toward the door blowing slow-motion kisses.

"Mama! Don't leave me! Mama! Mama!"

Her cool hand covers my forehead. "Wake up, Dory."

"What?"

"You were having a bad dream."

"Where's Byron?" The motel room comes into focus. Missy's in the mirror.

"Outside with Robert. It's time for breakfast." She smooths back my damp bangs. "My, that must've been a bad one."

"It was awful, Mama. Byron was lost—"

"What's so awful about that?" Missy says.

"—and you were léaving. There was a man by the window. I couldn't see his face—" But I've lost Mama. I can't keep her. She's rising.

"Hurry, Dory."

I drag myself out of bed and dress, slipping on my trusty one-way windows.

"Dory." Mama sighs. "Why do you wear those glasses? You have such pretty brown eyes."

"You never told me that before."

"If I said what I think, I'd always be talking." She slicks on her lipstick. "Let's go, girls."

And it's out of the air-conditioning and into the fire. Las Vegas shimmers and sizzles. Byron's an oasis in his green Hawaiian shirt, chewing a blade of grass he found heaven knows where, probably in the gift shop.

"You don't look too good," he says.

"I had this dream—"

It clings to me, unshakable, clammy, all through breakfast in the pink and orange restaurant, and on the road, the miles burning up beneath us. Byron and I hold hands, which we seldom do; only at really scary movies or when something atrocious happens. I wish I could curl up beside him and fall asleep—and Mama and Robert could be together, and Missy could be their little girl.

Were Missy's first words really "That's entertainment!"? Did she wake up one morning and say, "I want to be a star!"? Maybe some kids know what they mean to do. Maybe some know from birth, like Jesus. But most of us just want to grow up in peace—and they won't let us.

I knew this girl in school, Emmie Campbell. She's not there anymore. I liked her a lot. We ate lunch together, and she came to all my birthday parties.

One day, about eighth grade, while we were getting dressed for gym, I noticed these big red marks on her back. Welts. I'd always wondered what welts were. Emmie said yeah, her folks did that with a belt when they were drinking, which, unfortunately, was round the clock. I was shocked; her father owned the hardware store, and we were always running into her mom at the market. They never seemed drunk.

We talked about it sometimes, and I kept hoping the gym teacher would notice, but if she did, she never said anything to Emmie. Once I almost told Mama, but I stopped. The Campbells went to our church.

And Emmie—I don't know. She just looked at it as part of life: some people get blue eyes, some people get theirs blacked. There wasn't anything you could do about it. But in high school she got this terrible reputation because she went out to the parking lot at lunch and let all these guys screw her. I hate that word. And everyone put her down, but I still liked her because she was still Emmie, looking for love in the damnedest places. Then she got caught shoplifting and shipped to some detention home upstate, where she tried to slash her wrists with a broken light bulb, and that's the last I heard.

And everyone feels sorry for her parents.

But it's not just cannibals like the Campbells. It's the woman in the store embarrassed because her baby swore. "What did you say? What did you say?" He whispers it. WHACK. "We don't say that word!"

And Jeremiah getting whipped for seeing his mother with no clothes. He was four years old. The Reverend whipped him.

And Bobby's bloody Little League games. The coach foaming, the parents screaming. All those crying kids. "Are you thick, Woods? You should've caught that ball!" Bobby going after Coach Squatti with the bat.

And the time I almost got killed crossing the street, and Daddy was so relieved he almost killed me.

I'm not against adults; I plan to be one. I'm not against parents; they try. But sometimes instead of steering you safely through the jungle, they get bit by some exotic bug and decide you should be a model and starve you, or the main course, and stuff you . . . They've got the world's toughest job, next to growing up.

"Look!" Byron shouts.

In the distance we see a thick brown curtain. We part it and drive inside and there's Los Angeles. It's rush hour; the whole city is on the road, trying to get cross-town. We almost get killed. We tailgate at ninety. Everyone tailgates at ninety. Robert sips his Pepsi and slips from lane to lane, leaning on the horn when he has to.

One freeway leads to another and they're named instead of numbered, so if you don't know where you are, you never will. Robert points out the window; on a hill the word HOLLYWOOD shines like the star over Bethlehem. Missy almost jumps out.

There's more fast-food places than faces in the world: pizza, chicken, spuds, ribs, dogs. And rows of dirty pastel houses with patchy lawns or no lawns or crushed rock or Astroturf, and strange dream-colored science fiction flowers, and tortured cactuses, and dusty palms.

But no movie stars. That's a disappointment. We thought they lined the streets. We see some people who look like celebrities, but Robert says they're hoods.

We pass a studio; all you see is a giant locked gate, and a guard sitting behind it in a little house. Missy wants to stop and take the tour, but Robert says that's only for tourists.

And I remember that the main drawback with traveling is that once you leave home, you're a tourist; scorned by the locals as some separate, stupid species with nothing better to do than get lost and take pictures. When in reality we're all citizens of the world, but that would be difficult to explain to Robert.

We leave Hollywood and enter West Hollywood and turn down Lois Lane. It's full of ruts and rocks and junk, and a zillion yipping suicidal dogs trying to throw themselves under the Ford.

Then the road dead-ends at the Trail's End Trailer Park, which has a sign with one of those famous sagging Indians sitting on a hunched horse. We drive past rows of shining trailers packed like bullets in a box, till Robert stops in front of a blistered blue single-wide, and grinning says, "This is it."

"This is what?" Mama says blankly, blinking.

"Home sweet home. This is where I live."

"Robert, you never mentioned you live in a trailer." Mama's stunned. She thinks everyone who lives in trailers is somehow connected to the circus. Even Missy's stitched-on smile is puckering.

"Actually, I don't. I'm doing a friend a favor. The guy who owns this car. He and the wife were having some problems—"

"Who doesn't?" Mama says handsomely, rallying.

"—so they're staying at my house for a while and I'm staying here. It's really quite comfortable. You'd be surprised."

"I'm sure."

We get out and begin to unload the car. A few dusty kids come by to watch. Missy pounces on them hungrily and dazzles them with her batons. They ask if they can touch her hair, but she says no.

Robert unlocks the door, and the trailer breathes

fire. He turns on a small fan that blows the heat around. He offers us Pepsi from an otherwise bare fridge and hums while he draws up the grocery list.

"You make yourselves at home and I'll be back in a flash."

"We'll have everything put away," Mama promises proudly.

Which takes no time at all because there's no place to put anything. The bedroom me and Mama and Missy share is the size of my closet back home, and Byron's suitcase fills the room he shares with Robert. There's also a living room—make that livroom, and a cupboard of a kitchen and a tiny little bathroom where you can sit on the john, open the window, scrub the sink and turn on the shower simultaneously—but you can't turn around.

But it's clean, as Mama points out repeatedly. Besides, it's only temporary. Before you know it, Missy will buy Beverly Hills and kick everyone else out. I try to point out that *everything's* only temporary, but Missy's accordion overwhelms me.

[II]

We've spent the last eight days straight with Robert and really don't know him at all, I'm thinking, gazing at him across the breakfast tabl–there's no room for an *e*. For all we know he could be a mass murderer, though he doesn't have the eyes. Psychotic eyes look like open sores, and Robert's are as soft and brown as two Hershey kisses—and gazing right back at me.

"Penny for your thoughts, Dory."

"Nothing. I was just thinking."

"She's always thinking about nothing." Missy chortles around her cinnamon toast.

It's a comfort to know he can be so beautiful and still be polite. Ugly people *have* to be nice, whereas pretty people can get away with murder. They've got it made. Though once in a while you hear some beauty queen say how terrible it is, because men are afraid of you and women are jealous. I don't know. I wouldn't mind being prettier, though deep in my heart I know I should love myself the way I am, blahblahblah.

"Morning, people!" Mama's fresh as a flower from her shower. Tendrils of hair curl softly at her cheeks. Byron tips an imaginary hat.

"Mornin', Miss Scarlett."

"I'll take that as a compliment, Byron, whatever you meant."

She's very gay. In fact, she reminds me of the way she acts at barbecues after some beer.

"Sleep well, Lorraine?" Robert inquires.

"Like a baby. I feel positively rejuvenated!" She digs into her grapefruit, savoring each segment.

Missy makes an announcement. "Now that we're in California, I want everyone to call me Desiree. That goes for you and Birdbrain, Doris."

"Yassum, Miss Missy," Byron says.

"Missy's a lovely name," Robert says mildly, "but you're the boss."

"Not at all, Robert. You know best. After all, you're my manager."

Good luck. That's like managing Mighty Joe Young.

"I've been plotting our plan of attack," Robert says briskly. "First, I'll make a few phone calls, set up some auditions. Then"—he claps his hands and grins—"I'm going to show you folks the town. What will it be first?"

"Disneyland!" Missy shrieks.

"The ocean," I say simultaneously.

"Oh, Dory. It's just a bunch of water."

"Disneyland first is like dessert before dinner!"

"That doesn't make sense. You sound just like your poems."

"Let's take a vote," Mama says, which is a waste of time, because she sticks with Missy, Byron sticks with me, and Robert goes into the bedroom to make his calls. He won't take sides. Our family always takes sides, like tag-team wrestling.

Then I do something surprising. I *refuse* to go to Disneyland. Which is weird, because I want to see it, but I *have* to see the ocean. I hear it calling my name: *Dorothea* . . . If I said that, Mama and Missy would *really* think I'm nuts. Which they do anyway; it's in their eyes. If crossed, she might crack up. Who knows? I might.

I say, "You go to Disneyland, we'll go to the ocean."

"How will you get there?"

"Hitch."

"Doris Jane Woods! You'll do no such thing!"

"I was just kidding, Mama."

"Well, don't."

"We'll take the bus," Byron says. "Robert will tell us how to get there."

Which he does, though he seems genuinely disappointed we won't be joining them. But not too disappointed; he's bursting with good news. He's scheduled three auditions for Missy: two for commercials and one for a movie! How will she *wait* until tomorrow?

He drops us off at the bus stop, along with a map and a sack of oatmeal cookies. They drive away, not looking back, and the bus finally comes and we get on it.

It's all buses everywhere: big, smelly, full of nuts; punks pushing each other around and old folks in winter coats. We cross foreign country. Televisionland. The streets are paved with cars. We pass millions of shopping complexes, auto part places and liquor warehouses. How can there be so many stores? The sky's the color of old underwear. The air brown-blankets the hills. Robert said in case of a smog alert we should get inside and breathe as little as possible.

So many people. We'll never see them again. They get on and off the bus, fight over parking spaces, kiss, eat ice cream, shop and scratch.

It's hot. The bus drones on and on. I try to picture the ocean in my mind, but all I come up with is flat fields of corn rippling green to the horizon. And I'm afraid; afraid it will be smaller than my longing. Another disappointment.

But it's not.

Speechless, we get off the bus. We're all alone with the sea. It's gray, green, mother-of-pearl, the color of morning sky. I've never seen such color in my life, but I knew it existed. I knew.

We step out of our shoes in unison, leaving them far behind. The sand bakes the bottoms of our feet. The waves pound the beach, pound the beach.

Sea gulls screaming. Byron laughing, dizzy with the smell of the sea. Splashing, we race the thundering waves; slick with suntan oil and sweat, our hair stiff with salt. How will I describe this to Laurie? *Big, wet, blue* . . . She'll say: "Big, wet, blue! That sounds just like my brother! What was it *like?*" And I'll say:

Big, wet, blue . . .

"I don't know if you've noticed," Byron says, "but everyone here is nude."

We've been walking for miles and have stumbled across a white cove thick with fine sand and brown bodies; sunning, jogging, bobbing in the surf. Dogs bark and chase Frisbees.

We walk, the shore spins out before us like a ribbon on the gift of the sea. And my body, that fragile, flabby cross, falls away and I'm running free.

[12]

Sunset on the sea. Tangerine bleeds on the horizon. A black man and his black dog jog by the water's edge, sealed in shadow.

"What am I going to do, Byron?"

"About what?"

"Everything."

"Care to narrow that down?"

"You know. Them. My family. I feel so—"

"Homicidal?"

"Homesick. I guess that's it. Is it possible to miss Deadwood?"

"Anything's possible," Byron says. His baggy white pants blush with sunset. He looks exactly *right*. The wide-brimmed hat that drives Mama so wild looks custom-made by God.

"We should go soon. Mama will be frantic."

"Mama's always frantic," Bogie says.

"I don't know what to do lately. Everything's so weird."

"Like a dream come true."

"That's just it! It's too perfect! What was Robert really doing in Deadwood?"

"Knocking over a gas station, probably . . . I don't know. He seems like a nice guy, all things considered. He's very polite."

"Politeness isn't everything."

"No, but it makes up for a lot."

"Byron—"

"I agree with you, Dory! It's all very weird. Personally, I have no idea why we're here. But we are, and I'm having a good time, aren't you?"

"Yes, but—"

"Yes, but *what?*"

"I keep thinking about the future."

"Well, don't," Byron says. "It's a bad habit."

"But what's going to happen? Will Missy be a star?"

"I don't know, Dory. I just know we're here. Look where we are. Did you ever think you'd see this?"

He turns my face to the misty sea. It's too pretty to be real. If I painted what I see, Missy would say, "Clouds aren't that color." But they are.

"What am I going to do, Byron?"

"About what?"

"About my life. I have no idea what I'm supposed to do after we graduate."

"You can be a poet."

"How? You can't make any money at it till you're dead. What do I do in the meantime? Live at home? A few more years there and I'll be eating the wallpaper."

"Don't exaggerate, Dory. You're too sturdy for melodrama."

"Thanks heaps."

"I meant it as a compliment."

"Since when is fat a compliment?"

"You're not fat! Besides, we're talking fiber, not flab."

"I don't know *what* we're talking about. All I know is, the only normal person there is Bobby, and they treat him like yesterday's news."

Byron chews his blade of grass. "I think Bobby has that covered."

"Why should he cover anything? That's his home!"

"Sounds very homey."

"Byron, you're deliberately missing the point!"

"You know I'm not. That's just the way it is."

"Well, that explains everything."

"What's to explain? Your folks are a little nuts. Who isn't?"

How can you argue with logic like that? Besides, I know he's right. It could be worse. Our parents don't beat us. They just kind of forget we're there. If it's not Missy, or on TV, it's not real; they don't see it. Which brings me to something else: if I were happy, could I write? Most of my poetry comes from the blues, but I can't see depression as a career. Not that all writers are alcoholics or jump off cliffs—just the ones they make movies about.

And if the truth be known—as it eventually must—

I know exactly what I mean to do with my life. It scares me just to think of it. I can hear Daddy now—

I want to be a minister, in the Church of the True Believer, nationwide membership 2 million 332 thousand souls, give or take a few. There are no women ministers in the Church of the True Believer, and when the subject comes up, as it does with increasing frequency, Reverend Roy rages purple from the pulpit.

"If our beloved Saviour hadn't resurrected, He'd be spinning in His grave! A woman's place is in the home! Not in the ministry, or the Congress, or the United States Army, but in the home, where God intended! If He said it once, He said it a million times: 'A woman's place—' "

He never said it. We're equal in His eyes. But lest the Reverend be thought prejudiced, it should, in all fairness be pointed out that he hates everyone alike: young and old, rich and poor, man, woman and child. We're too human.

"And those who oppose Him shall burn in—" There's no Hell, except in his mind. Anyway, it'd be Standing Room Only, because he's got it packed to the rafters with Catholics, Buddhists, Presbyterians, Jews— in other words, anyone who's not a True Believer.

"The Good Lord will forgive me when I say I'd rather see a woman fry in flames than serve as a minister in this church!"

God help me, I want to sow hope and love and joy. I want to be an antidote to the poison.

Dory, have you lost your mind? I can picture my

parents' faces. I haven't even told Byron yet, which makes me feel like a traitor.

I thought the Call came like a knock at the door: "Telegram for Dory Woods!" But it's not a knock; it's a small, sure voice, winking like a tiny flame. I've tried to smother it; it won't go out. Is it you, Lord, or craziness? How can I be sure? Why must I always ask for a sign, a shiny arrow pointing the way?

"Byron?"

"What?"

I fill my hands with sand. "I want to be a minister."

He considers this. "It costs two bucks."

"You know what I mean. Don't laugh."

"Who's laughing?" His calm gray eyes warm my face. "The day you take the pulpit is the day I'll go to church."

"Byron Spears! You said you'd never go to church."

"Doris Jane, I never say never no more."

We hold hands. It's good to have someone to touch in this world. Little kids have it, and married folks too, but in between can be lonesome. That's why I always wanted a dog, but Daddy's allergic and Mama hates a mess, so I had to make do until Byron. Dear Byron.

We'll never see the ocean for the first time again. I feel as though I've lost and found it. If I died this moment, I'd die complete, my eyes full of the sea.

"We better go." Byron hauls me to my feet and we turn toward the highway.

[13]

Dear Bobby,

This will be short since Missy's tugging on my writing arm and will eventually pull it out of the socket and I'll have to quit. She's anxious to get to her audition, but Mama's not nearly ready. She's trying on one outfit after another. You'd think it was *her* audition. It's for a remake of some Shirley Temple movie. Don't ask me why they're doing it twice.

What day is this? Monday? I'm losing track of time. We've gone into another dimension. Anyway, I'd swear it's August. Happy August, Bobby.

Well, California's just like we pictured it. Especially L.A. Byron calls it Lower Alabama, but it's not so bad. It's a smiling orange wearing sunglasses and a woman's bikini'd body, if that makes sense. Byron fits.

He looks like a native. No wonder he sticks out in Oklahoma.

It's warm and sunny and expensive and the people are tanned and loud, except for the tourists, who are sunburned and shy. Missy's gone crazy. It's like she's plugged in. She actually believes she's Desiree Jones and is all the time smiling and flexing her dimples.

But outside of that, everyone's fine. You should see me; I've lost five pounds. I had to, to live in the trailer. Bobby, there are worse things than Robert's trailer but only quicksand comes to mind. It's like living in a lunchbox. The only time I'm alone is in the john, and Missy's forever pounding on the door. There seems to be some sort of psychic link between us.

Mama and Robert took Missy to Disneyland. She had a wonderful time. Mickey Mouse came over and kissed her hand, which she took as a sign. She described the day down to the striped straw in her soda, so I don't know as By and I'll need to go. We went to the ocean instead. Bobby, I wish you could've seen it. It's just as good as we thought it would be, only ten times better. I bought some postcards of it but they look so dead; I'll send them along anyway.

The other day we saw some people called Dykes on Bykes. You'd have loved it, Bob; all these Marlon Brando women on big Harleys with their girlfriends in back. You should've heard Missy. You know how she is: Hanging's too good for them, etc. etc. They're probably nice enough people.

Then Robert took us to lunch in a neighborhood

downtown where every day is Halloween: most of the women you see are men, and the men are really women. People kept approaching Robert, and this one guy— Bobby, he was seven feet tall, wearing an itty-bitty biker jacket with a winged skull in back—he went for me. Didn't talk; just grinned and drooled. We lost him in a Doggie Diner.

I also saw the most beautiful woman. She looked like a fairy princess. She was standing on the curb as if she'd just stepped out of a pumpkin, in a sky-blue taffeta dress, her long hair curling just right. (Unlike mine. Bobby, how come my hair only looks good when nobody else is around?) But I kept having the feeling something about her was different; you know, what's wrong with this picture? And it turned out to be her goatee, which I hadn't even noticed, he was so beautiful . . . I know that doesn't make sense, Bob. Nothing does. This whole trip is like a hallucination. The weather's too good, the people are too nice. The TV stations stay on all night. *There's no night here.* Just station breaks. Mama has the set on at six-thirty every morning, pacing around drinking too much coffee. Her favorite show is *Bewitched* but she's partial to Mr. Ed. This morning he wrote a song, and a publisher thought it might be a hit.

We had a publicity stunt the other day. Robert arranged it. Missy was supposed to be like Judy Garland in *The Wizard of Oz*. A hot-air ballon was going to land in the park and carry her away, and Robert rented this little dog and everything.

But it turned out the hot-air man couldn't make it, and a *helicopter* showed up instead, almost *decapitating* this guy walking his great Dane. Then the police came and bawled out Robert; and the rented dog, this vicious little terrier, took a chunk out of Missy's leg. *She picked him up and bit him* at the exact moment that the only reporter who'd bothered to show up took a picture. It made the *Times*, page three, captioned: "Bow-OW!" Missy cried when she saw it. I said it was better than no publicity at all, but Mama wouldn't let me keep the picture.

I've got to go, Bob. Mama's finally ready. I don't know when we'll be home. Robert says these things take time, but I think his idea of time and Missy's idea are different. She wouldn't hang around a half-hour for the Second Coming. She wants it all NOW.

Nuts. She just read that part over my shoulder and is really having a fit.

"*I'm* having a fit, huh? Look who's talking! The only reason you and Birdbrain got to come is because you were having such a *cow* about it!"

Moooo. Take care, Bobby. Give my love to Daddy and tell him everything's fine. Who knows? Maybe it is.

Your loving sister,
Dory

[14]

The Hotel Roscoe's ballroom is huge and usually packed with dancing debs or conventioneers in silly hats and name tags that say HELLO! I'M DRUNK! But today it hosts five hundred Shirley Temple clones. It's staggering.

Byron makes his *Twilight Zone* sound effect: asphyxiating violins.

"Cram it, Birdbrain," Missy says half-heartedly. The rest of us are speechless.

It's a dream; it's a scene from an old cartoon, one of those frightening factories: kids rolled off an assembly line like so many manic dolls.

"Shoot!" Mama shouts over a thousand tap shoes. "You're the cutest, Baby." But Missy doesn't look too sure. She clings to Robert's Mr. Roarke suit, his tanned hand resting on her hair.

This last week wasn't good. Nobody called back after Missy's auditions. Robert's phone never rings, except at two in the morning; a woman named Sylvia, who screams. Robert insists it's a crank call. Then Sylvia *really* screams.

He herds us to a table manned by a woman who looks like a drowned Kewpie doll. The bouf's gone out of her bouffant and her mascara's headed south.

"Name?" She stabs her cigarette into a smoldering face-shaped ashtray. Then she gets a good look at Robert. "Name?" she leers between coughs.

"Missy Woods," Mama says.

"Desiree Jones," Missy says simultaneously.

"Missy, we've been through this!"

"It's *my* career!"

"Put down Missy Woods for now," Robert says calmly. The woman does his bidding. Who wouldn't? He's dazzling in his ice cream suit, as if he carried word from the gods, or tidings of a new, improved detergent.

In the background a kid is firing her father.

"Age?"

"Nine," Mama says.

"Ten," Missy says.

"Nine and a half," Robert tells the woman.

"Experience?"

Missy begins to recite her recitals, but Robert cuts in, cool as a cuke, and tells about the TV commercials she made for a used car dealer in Tulsa. Not to mention the time she entertained the governor. Mama doesn't bat a lash.

"It'll be a while," the woman says, stifling a yawn or a sob. "You're number 432."

"That's my lucky number!" Missy twinkles, but the woman doesn't notice.

There's no place to sit. We press down front to the stage. There's a kid on it and a not-so-grand piano, pounded by a retired heroin addict.

The kid's a carbon copy of Missy, down to her embroidered anklets. In a tiny, goldfish voice she sings, "Getting to know you, getting to know all about you; Getting to like you, getting to hope you like—"

"Next!" a man hollers. "Thanks, honey."

Crushed, the kid scrapes herself offstage. The man, Robert calls him the casting director, whispers to his assistant. She scribbles in her notebook then shouts, "Number 403, please!"

"Mama!" Missy says. "I have to go!"

"You just went. Relax your muscles."

"Relaxing won't help!"

"Yes it will. It's all in your mind."

"It's *not* in my mind! And in a minute it'll be on your shoes!"

"Melissa Jean Woods!"

"Well, gol! I have to go!"

"Don't let us keep, you," Byron says.

"Go with her, Dory."

"I don't need to go."

"Don't argue. Just step on it."

Dismal thought.

We hurry to the giant, mirrored john, where Missy cuts in line in front of a kid who looks just like her.

"Hey!" the kid says, beating on the door. "It's not your turn!"

"Sit on it," Missy says from inside the stall.

I fight through the crush of clones and moms and squeeze onto a cracked vinyl couch next to a pile of sobbing clothing that turns out to be Number 402.

"It'll be okay," I say, a preposterous lie. Fortunately, she doesn't hear me.

Missy comes out and stares at the kid. Then she does something amazing. She kneels and knocks on the kid's head.

"Knock, knock," she says, pushing aside the tangled curls, revealing bruised blue eyes. "Don't do that. You'll wreck your makeup."

"Everything's wrecked already!" the kid sobs, trying to turn away.

"No it's not. This is one audition. Don't take it so hard."

She pats the kid's head, and we walk out. I'm so touched I try to hug her.

"Quit it, Dory. You're smushing my dress."

We find Robert. It's not hard; everyone over ten is staring at him. He looms like a gorgeous lighthouse; so calm, so elegantly casual. Sometimes he's so casual he seems dead, vampirical. I half expect to wake up some night with Missy fastened to my neck. How can he be so cool when everything's so weird? Maybe it's *not* that weird. Maybe it's me.

"Are you okay, Dory?" he inquires kindly. "You look a little pale."

"It's her natural color," Missy says. "Geez, I gotta go again!"

"You stay here! It's almost your turn!"

"I can't, Mama!"

"I'll take her." Robert tucks Missy under his arm and parts the crowd like a fullback.

"Number 429!"

Mama lights another cigarette. She's just started smoking. Daddy wouldn't approve. I wonder if she'll smoke when we go back to Oklahoma. I wonder if we'll ever go back again.

"Number 432!"

Robert bursts through the crowd and deposits Missy onstage. She changes; I can't explain it, but she changes. Her face sharpens, congeals.

" 'Cry Me A River,' " she tells the pianist.

"Say what?"

"You heard me."

He shrugs and pounds it out.

Is Missy good? I don't know. She's too close to come into focus. But compared to the last ten contestants, she's a smash. They let her finish the song.

"Honey, would you tell us a little bit about yourself?"

Only too happy to oblige, she prattles prettily; Heidi on speed. Robert tenses like a fishing reel beside me. Her hobbies are dancing and dressing her dolls. Her favorite color is pink. Her—

"Thanks, honey. That's fine."

But something's changed. Robert's antennae are

twitching. He lifts her down from the stage and confronts the casting director.

"Excuse me. The name is Robert Banks. I represent Miss Woods."

"What can we do for you, Banks?" The man sighs. "You can see we're kind of backed up."

"I just wanted to thank you for taking an interest in Missy. We're awfully proud of this little girl."

"She's cute," the man says, "but she won't work out."

"Why not?" Robert asks abruptly.

"The accent."

"The what?"

"The accent. You could cut it with a knife."

A terrible tragedy takes place on Robert's face. Tilt signs light up in his eyes. The roaring in his ears is almost audible.

"Robert?" Mama's lost, frightened. Her hand goes to her throat. That's a thing she does when she's nervous, to keep the real words from coming out. "What does he mean? What should we do?"

He forces up the corners of his mouth. "We should go home and have lunch. I'm starved."

"But the accent—What was he talking about?"

His hands flutter up and massage his temples. "It seems," he says slowly, "that Missy sounds southern. Somehow I never noticed. Silly me."

"I didn't mean to!" Missy blurts, on the verge of tears.

"It's not your fault, Baby," Mama says. "Everything's going to be fine."

But she doesn't say fine—she says fahn. And Missy's not nine—she's nahn. And suddenly I notice we're *all* doing it, all of us except Robert.

"Incredible," Byron says.

Mama corks him with a look. "Well, it's not the end of the world! Missy's such a bright little thing! (Thang.) In no time at all we'll have her talking like a native."

"Pygmy?" Byron says.

By the time we get back to the trailer, Robert's laughing and promising next time we'll go the distance. He sends me and Byron out for Missy's favorite ice cream, Peach Passion. It has little chunks of peach and gum and nuts in it. It looks already ate.

I hear Mama on the phone to Daddy.

"Wey, you would've been so proud! Baby almost got the part, except for this little technicality . . . I don't know, hon. These things take time. Of course I miss you, too."

[15]

One thing you can say about Robert: he doesn't drink.

Just Pepsi, about five gallons a day. Byron says the carbonation has somehow affected Robert's mind and made him *think* he's a Hollywood agent when in reality he's who-know's-what. I doubt that he means us any harm. Underneath the layers of Old Spice and bull, he probably thinks he's doing us a favor . . . Just the way he thinks he's an agent.

It's nutty around here. Missy all the time in front of the mirror, smiling and practicing her new accent. Robert on the phone, alphabetically working his way through the directory. And Mama—she's started drinking, but she doesn't notice because she's drinking. Not much; she's one of those people who looks at a bottle and giggles. Two tiny glasses of Sangria and Mama's in the islands.

"Change the channel, Dory."

"But we want to watch the news."

"It's the same every night. I'm so sick of rape and murder."

"But, Mama—"

"If the world ends, your daddy will let us know. Change the channel."

So I change it, hurrying past *Gilligan's Island*, which Missy will scream for if she sees it's on, till I get to channel 55, which only shows programs, mostly comedies, made before that year. Just as I get there, a commercial ends and an oily voice says, ". . . so you don't have to think about it."

"Exactly." Mama settles herself with a fresh glass, then *Love American Style* comes on.

She's real depressed lately. Cynical and sarcastic. It's a switch from the pom-pom routines, but worse. The last time she got this way was when John Wayne died. She was a big fan, as in fanatic. Would've voted for him if he'd run for president. I never cared for his movies much; but on the other hand, he was always the same: he never changed horses and fooled you. His real name was Marion Something, and he wasn't a sheriff or a soldier, just an actor. But try telling that to my mother. She felt the same way about Elvis.

"He was so young!" she said over and over. "There'll never be anyone like him!" But there doesn't need to be, because it's like they never die. They'll live forever in reruns.

I think she misses my father, too. They've slept in the same bed for nineteen years, longer than I've been alive. I wonder how he and Bobby are making out. It's hard to picture them at the dinner table without Mama translating. Daddy's probably working lots.

"Who cares about split ends?"

"What's that, Mama?"

But she's just talking back to the set. "So let him make his *own* coffee! What *will* you do? What WILL you DO?"

This is such a stupid show. I hate canned laughter. All those faceless hyenas killing themselves. But there's always the chance something good might come on, so we stay tuned, hour after hour, until suddenly it's time to go to bed. Another wasted evening at #47, Trail's End Trailer Park, West Hollywood.

Maybe I'm overreacting the way they say I do. Making a big deal about nothing. No. The TV's always on and my mother's always bickering with it. But it's like it's alive; we can't turn it off for fear we'll offend it. The other night Byron fell down in front of the set, screaming: "I can't do it! I can't kill it! Don't make me turn it off!"

"For heaven's sake, Byron! Act like a grown-up," Mama said.

I wish I could be like Byron. He's like Robert, without the secrets. So calm; the eye of the hurricane while the rest of us blow around him. He called home the other night. The conversation went like this:

BYRON: Right, Dad. *That* Byron. How's it going? How's Mom? . . . That's too bad. What's the doctor

[94]

sav? . . . . Aunt Who did what? How was the funeral?
. . . That's nice. No, nothing much. Just wanted to let
you know I'm still alive . . . They're fine. Missy almost got this Shirley Temple part—Missy. The little
one, yeah. But she has this accent—an Oklahoma accent,
Dad.´ Uh-huh . . . Well, say hi to Mom. I hope she's
better soon . . . No, that won't be necessary, Dad.
Really, I've got plenty. Fine, I'll be expecting it. Bye.

And hung up smiling.

I'm worried all the time. My stomach's in knots.
I'm worried about Mama and Robert. After all, she's
a very attractive woman, and he's a perfectly attractive
man. So perfect he could've been assembled from spare
parts in the Leading Man bin at Central Casting.

What will happen? Is it possible they've already
made love? No. For one thing, there isn't room in the
trailer, and for another, Mama's not the type. But she's
thinking about it, I can tell. Constantly checking her
hair and slicking her lips.

I'm afraid she'll go crazy if she sleeps with him. She
has real concrete ideas about right and wrong. Concrete
as in cement. If she did, she'd feel so guilty I just know
she'd do something rash: like tell my father, or overdose
on Sleep-Eze, or tattoo a scarlet A on her chest and join
the Hell's Angels.

On the other hand, if this tension keeps up, she'll
crack, so it's all the same. I can't change Mama and am
beginning to wonder why I try. Things could be
worse. Someday I'll embroider that on a sampler. Ev-

eryone has some little quirk, and Missy just happens to be Mama's. It's not that she's dumb; far from it. She just can't see around the stars in her eyes. Mama lives on dreams, and me and Bobby are real. She's quietly proud of us. I wish she could be loudly proud but she can't, so what's the point.

I haven't written any poetry lately. Got too much on my mind. All I've come up with are a few Hints for Heloise. Bobby will get a bang out of them.

Dear Heloise,

Here is a wonderful new use I have discovered for your column. I shred it into teeny little pieces and put it in my canary's cage. He is a great fan of yours and never misses your column.

Dory Woods, age 87½

Dear Heloise,

Here is a helpful hint for using your column in the Sunday paper. First, separate the comic section from the sports, the news, etc. Then carefully roll, starting at one end, into a long, cylindrical tube, being careful not to crease or tear. Now, hit flies with it! Smashing!

Mrs. Bubba Peterson

My little boy Brock, aged 4½, used to love to help me make cookies. He'd sit on the counter while I cut them out, throw dough, get flour on his clothes, and in general make a big mess. But not anymore! I took one of my old plastic bread bags and put it over his head. I have not heard from him since.

Jojo Houston

Me and Byron also wrote a hit song. If Mr. Ed can do it, so can we. It's called "It's Only Trash, But That's What You Love." We sent it to a publisher downtown. We figure it'll sell a million copies.

Mama says not to let my imagination run away with me, but she's the one running wild in her mind down streets of stars with Missy's face on each one. Daddy's no better. Sometimes I think this whole thing started when he got Danny Kaye's autograph on their honeymoon.

This feels like the time we got lost when I was little. We were on our way to the fair. I didn't know fathers could get lost; I cried and cried. Eventually we got there, but I've never been the same.

The walls are wavy, the floor is gone. We're floating free in space. How can I possibly plan ahead when I have no idea what will happen next? Missy could become a superstar or be trampled into the ground. Mama could become an alcoholic or a talk-show panelist. Robert could turn out to be a genuine agent or a genuine lunatic. Will it be door number one, two or three? Every time I hear Bobby's voice on the phone, I want to crawl through the wires and be with him, he's so sane. California's strange, but mostly it's my family. If it weren't for Byron, I'd be alone in this sunny mob.

It's Only Trash, But That's What You Love

You used to dance to raunch-and-roll, baby,
Do you remember when?
Then you discovered soul, baby,
I loved to love you then.
But now you glitter like a falling star,
You can't remember who you really are,
It's only trash, but baby, that's what you love.

It's okay to wear high heels, baby,
You can take the fall.
Wear a dead cat on your head now, baby,
I'll accept it all.
But when you tell me that it's really Art,
You blow my mind and you break my heart.
It's only trash, but baby, that's what you love.

The world is old and moldy, baby,
There's really nothing new.
You think you're Now; you're just an oldy, baby,
Something bored and blue.

But when the sequins start to fall,
I'll be there to catch them all,
It's only trash, but baby, that's what you love.

[16]

Missy got on the *Tonight Show!* I saw it, but I still don't believe it. They saw her picture in the paper biting the dog and had to have her. That's the kind of show it was.

Johnny wasn't there. That awful Wink Dixon was the guest host, and he just about makes me sick. The only reason people laugh at his jokes is that he cries if they don't.

Mama and Robert got to go backstage. Byron and I sat in the audience. It looked a lot different than it does on TV; the studio was small, the set was made of cardboard, and a little sign told us when to applaud. Fortunately for Wink, it was the kind of crowd that when you said New Jersey, they roared.

While the cameras rolled, Wink screamed and laughed and pretended his desk was a boat. But every time they went to a commercial, he collapsed like a broken-down boxer. Then six guys would rush out and massage his wrists and pour stuff down his throat.

Missy followed a singing dog act. She wore her

silver-spangled drum majorette outfit and did a tap and baton routine to "Send In The Clowns," which, up until that moment, was one of my very favorite songs.

The audience loved her. They clapped and clapped. Then Wink made her sit on his lap, and in this awful baby-talk voice he asked wasn't it hard for a little bitty girl like her to perform in front of thirty million people? Missy considered this for a second or two, then said, "You know, Wink, it's like the Good Book says: We have nothing to fear but ourselves."

Then she had a sleazy conversation with an obscene ventriloquist's dummy. I mean the dummy was obscene; the ventriloquist was mental. All I could think of was a *Twilight Zone* episode where the dummy took over the man and had him committing murder and madness. This was the kind of dummy that would think up stuff like that. It had big round eyes and a Beatle haircut and made suggestive remarks to Missy while its owner rolled his eyes and giggled.

Finally the show was over. Wink said, "Remember, ladies and gentlemen, if God hadn't meant us to laugh, He wouldn't have invented the whoopie cushion!" And stood and took a tremendous bow and collapsed on his desk. Curtain.

Afterwards, there was a party backstage. We drank warm champagne and ate old strawberries. Robert took pictures of Missy with the other guests: a football player, a champion cow-chip tosser, the singing dog and the dummy and his manager. To hear Mama talk, it was the Show of the Century. We called Daddy. He was dazzled. He's under the impression Missy's just a baby-step from the big time.

The next day we celebrated. It was exhausting.

On the way to Disneyland (Missy's choice), we got stuck inside a huge Hell's Angels parade. There must've been two hundred of them, broiling in black leather.

Robert stayed cool as a clam till the horn jammed. Usually it stops in a minute or two. Mama finally said, "What's wrong?"

He slapped the steering column. "It won't stop."

"Is he serious?" Missy said.

"Robert, are you serious?"

"I'm afraid so, Lorraine." The horn blared and blared. He gestured helplessly, mimed total frustration. The bikers didn't smile back.

"This is very awkward." Mama plucked at her throat. A biker kicked her door.

"Mama!" Missy screamed suddenly. "I'm scared!"

"Jumpin' Judas, don't *do* that, Missy! You just took ten years off my life!"

"Well, geez! What's going to happen?"

"They'll probably eat us," Byron said. "We'll be famous missing persons, like Judge Crater and Amelia Earhart."

"Sure, look on the bright side," I said.

"Can't you two see we're having a crisis? Robert, can't you fix it?"

"Must be a short." He beat the steering wheel.

Byron said, "You ought to give this car back to

your friends. You know, the people who own the trailer."

"I can see why they were having problems!" Mama snapped. The biker near her window licked his lips.

"Just calm down, everyone. Just calm down." Smiling and waving, Byron hung out the window, doing his Jimmy Stewart.

"It's the horn, fellas! Horn's stuck! Can't make the goshdarn thing stop!" Then he pointed to Robert and circled his ear with his finger. The bikers roared off.

"Your Stewart's very good," Robert said. The horn stopped. We got to Disneyland.

Missy took it upon herself to be our guide. She wouldn't let us do anything we wanted to. Unfailingly, she steered us to the rides with the longest lines, snaking up and down and all around, then the ride would last two minutes.

It was very clean. An army of apple-cheeked boys and girls stabbed litter to death everywhere you looked. Dixie music and bird calls blared from trees, which were so lifelike it was astonishing they were real. It was hot and crowded. Everyone wore funny tee shirts: "I'm Goofy for Disneyland!" "Kiss Me! I'm Really a Handsome Prince!" We walked a million miles, but mostly it was fun. My favorite ride was the Matterhorn. I love to hear Missy scream.

Then we went home, and Robert made tacos with avocados, tomatoes and garbanzo beans. He has a saying: "Don't panic; it's organic." I'm not sure how Pepsi fits into that, but the other night Mama made one of her famous Sweetie Pies: crushed Oreos crust, butterscotch pudding and Hippolite dotted with maraschino cherries, and Robert just about had an attack.

After supper Mama sent me and Byron out for Peach Passion. The ice cream store guy didn't even ask, just started dishing it up when he saw us coming.

When we got back, Mama was all dressed up in a glittery red tube top I'd never seen.

"I have wonderful news for you two! We're going dancing!"

Wonderful. Mama made me wear a dress. Byron put on a really good tie with painted palm trees he bought for fifteen cents.

Missy didn't shriek when we left. I wonder how they bribed her. Daddy wouldn't like us leaving her alone. He wouldn't like any of this.

I feel as if I'm falling down an elevator shaft—and Mama's falling up it. "Dory," she says, flying by me, "don't be such a dud." I keep falling and falling; there's nothing to grab onto. It'll almost be a relief to hit bottom.

Talk about your weird double-dates: Mama and Robert up front investing Missy's invisible money, me and Byron in back dissecting her invisible career. Robert took us to a place called Disco-Pacetic. A little creep outside was screening the guests.

Lots of people got turned away; too thin, too fat, too normal. Of course, when he saw Robert, we got in immediately. Robert's like the key to Oz.

Inside it was a Fellini movie. The Beautiful People at play. There were mirrors everywhere, filled with vacant faces. The dark throbbed with colored lights. The strobes gave Mama a terrible headache until she had some wine.

The machine-made music droned on and on, so loud I could feel it in my fillings, orchestrated by a demented deejay with delusions of talent, named Dr. Doom.

Robert and Mama danced. I mean like they were *born* to dance. I mean Fred Astaire and Ginger Rogers. It was beautiful and awful to see.

Mama loves to dance, and Daddy won't; he stands there, wooden, while she spins. But Robert—Robert was mercury; a silver stream surrounding her. She twirled in dizzy circles in his arms.

Byron and I didn't dance. I just sat there, watching Mama; her long hair lashing, face flashing in the strobe.

Finally Fred and Ginger were ready to go home. Every light in the trailer was on. Missy met us at the door, hysterical.

"What is it, Baby? Missy, what's wrong?"

Nothing. She was ecstatic.

"*Shoot for the Stars* called! They want me on the show!"

"Shoot. That's the tackiest program on TV."

"Butt out, Birdbrain. This is my big chance!"

Mama rushed to call Daddy.

As we got ready for bed, Missy said, "I'm going to be bigger than the *Titanic!*"

[17]

It's funny how you can know someone so long and so well you stop seeing them; they become an extension of you, like your arm. Like Byron.

Then suddenly everything's different; all the patterns are changed, and the labels are gone, and for an instant your eyes are wide open, and you *see*.

And you think about fortune and fate and chance. *What if I hadn't met Byron?* What if we were rolling around loose? I wouldn't have found him in anyone else. There's no one like him.

Seems as though we've known each other forever, but it's been five years. Bobby was sitting on him. Bobby was scary in those days. Running around mad all the time, he didn't know about what. Hurting. And there was Byron, decked out like a Christmas tree in the desert; the long hair, sandals, crazy shirts. Bobby landed on him, outside the school cafeteria.

Byron wasn't scared; didn't act it, anyway. He was

doing his John Wayne: "Come on, big fella, get up before you hurt yaself," etc.

I squeezed through the crowd around them and said, "Quit that, Bobby," and he did, and went off with his friends. Byron got up, and we walked off, talking, and haven't stopped since.

He's the best person I know, much nicer than I am. Lots of times I'm good because God's watching, and I want Him to say, "Doris Jane, aren't you something! I'm saving you a place by me."

But Byron—I don't know; he exists on another frequency. Smiling and laughing, but not like a lunatic; Byron's in love with living. His glass is half-full and mine is half-empty, and he's always got plenty for me.

Best of all, no matter what I say, no matter what I think, he loves me. Whoever I am, under all the disguises, that's who Byron sees.

And too often I don't even see him; I take him for granted, like breathing; busy waiting for the coming attractions to end so my real life can start. When in reality my life's going on *right now*, this minute, directed by and starring me. Thank God Byron's in it.

It's two o'clock in the morning. Everyone's in bed but him and me. The trailer's snug as a submarine, and just as separate from the world.

We watch TV. It's stupider than usual. Especially the commercials. A guy in a mask called the Loan Arranger invites us to borrow five thousand dollars. Two women discuss disposable diapers at their class reunion.

"Oh, you know what I want right now? One of

Mama's Sweetie Pies! Can't you just taste that marsh-mallow creme?"

"Thank my lucky star, no."

"Why do I like to eat so much? If food's the answer, what's the question?"

"Beats me. Anyway, you're doing good, Dory. Imagine how you would've handled the situation in the past."

"Which situation?"

"The one we're in with Robert. You would've eaten two tubs of Cool Whip."

The memory of it makes me gag. "You promised you'd never mention that! What can I say? Something was happening."

"Something's always happening," Byron says. "Now you're dealing with it positively."

"Right. I want to throw myself in the traffic."

"But you don't. That's the point. You're a survivor."

Am I? The word hovers in the air. I try it on. It fits. And for once I don't feel scared or depressed, and the only clock is the one in my breast. *I'm alive*—and I have to go to the john.

The light's so bright. I fear the mirror. But I face her, whoever she is, the stranger.

I realized something the other day: I have no idea what I look like. Pictures of me don't look like me to me, but everyone insists they're true. "There's nothing wrong with the camera," Missy says.

As a matter of fact, I'm a family joke. Seems when

I was six, I saw a picture of me and Bobby with the neighbor kids, and I pointed to myself and said, "Who's that?" Seeing yourself in a picture you come face-to-face with being alive. There you are, smiling and waving. It can come as kind of a shock.

Mirrors can be a shock, too. I'm never who I expect. I'm a daisy looking to be a rose. But I like daisies best.

I come back into the living room. For a second I see Byron: the long, blond hair, the baggy pants, the faded Hawaiian shirt. Beautiful.

He's looking at me, smiling. "Can I ask you something, Dory?"

"Sure." But my stomach tightens.

"Why do you wear your bangs so long? It's hard to see your eyes."

"That's why."

"Are you trying to keep stuff in or out?"

"Both. You're making me blush."

"That's why you wear those glasses."

"I lost those glasses."

"Congratulations."

I don't ever need to protect myself from Byron. I think I fully realized that this minute.

The Loan Arranger's on again. Byron says, "That guy sure looks like Robert."

"Oh, please. I can't think about Robert now. If I think about him—"

"—you'll start laughing hysterically, and your mother will rush out and demand an explanation, which you'll be incapable of furnishing."

"Quit now. Don't get me started."

"I love your laugh, Dory. It's contagious."

"You mean infectious."

"That too. You know, Robert might be exactly what he says he is."

"He never says."

"Exactly."

"Dory?" Mama calls from the bedroom.

"What is it, Mama? (See what you've done!)"

"Are you all right? What's so funny out there?"

"Nothing. It's this movie."

The most preposterous movie is on. It's called *Wild in the Streets* and was made back in 1968, when nothing made sense. It features tons of rampaging teenagers with Shemp haircuts taking over the country. They terrorize everyone over thirty-five with threats of death and sitar music and are constantly revolting, but it's so low-budget that the riot scenes are patched-in clips of the Boxer Rebellion.

"Look out, here comes the kitchen sink!" Byron says as Dick Clark makes a guest appearance. Shelley Winters, hamstrung on hashish, is the mother of "our" candidate for president: a maniac rock 'n' roll singer with the integrity of a jelly dougnut. Richard Pryor plays one of the dougnut's lieutenants. And Hal Holbrook fights a losing battle as the only brave congressman over thirty-five. Someone slips him LSD. His punk son tells him to sit on a happy face.

"Dory?"

"Mama! You startled me." Her presence changes the room.

Byron leaps up. "Goodnight, everybody. I'm going to bed."

The big chicken.

Mama pours a glass of wine. She hasn't been sleeping well lately; tosses and turns and gets up with Mr. Ed. For a while she was drinking too much coffee, her fingernails rattling on the formica. Now I put decaffeinated in the caffeinated jar. She's just as awake, but she doesn't twitch.

"What're you watching?"

"This really stupid movie."

"Sounds wonderful." She sits down. "What's it about?"

"A society where everyone over thirty-five is shot."

"Terrific. Hand me my cigarettes."

"You shouldn't smoke."

"I know that, Dory."

"It's self-destructive."

"I'll stop."

"When?"

"When things calm down! Will you stop with the questions? I swear, since you were a little child its been who, when, why. 'The pitter-patter of little lips,' Daddy used to say. Hand me the matches."

She lights up, coughing. She doesn't smoke well. Lord, I love my mother. I love her inside out. I wish there were some way to tell her so she'd know it in her heart.

The teenagers execute Shelley Winters. I say: "Mama, are you in love with Robert?"

Wine sprays out of her mouth and down the front of her robe.

"Doris Jane Woods! What kind of question is that?"

"I don't mean love. I mean sex. I mean—I don't know *what* I mean, Mama! I'm scared!"

"About what?" She fixes her face in a mask.

"About everything! This whole trip! It's like a situation comedy!"

"I don't know what you mean, Dory." She refills her glass.

"Look at us! Living in this trailer with some guy we don't even know—"

"Robert is Missy's manager. He's going to make her a star."

"Mama, you can't believe that."

"I *have* to. Otherwise, why are we here?"

"That's what I'm asking." I can't stop.

She lights another cigarette. "Don't you love your sister, Dory?"

"I'm trying."

"That's a strange thing to say."

"She's a strange kid."

"And I suppose that's my fault."

"I didn't say that, Mama."

"No, but that's what you're thinking. Let me tell

you something, Dory. Hand me that bottle."

"Mama—"

"Will you please remember that I'm the mother and you're the child? Do as I say."

I hand her the bottle. "I'm not a child."

She shakes her head. "I don't understand you, Dory. Why do you want to grow up so fast? There's plenty of time to accept responsibility. Believe me, that's all life is. You can't escape. Look at me: I'll be thirty-seven my next birthday. Do you realize what that means? I'm middle-aged. My life's half done."

"No it's not, Mama. You're pretty and smart—"

But she doesn't hear me.

"I had two babies by the time I was nineteen. Two years older than you. Can you imagine? I was just a baby myself but I did the best I could, and sometimes that wasn't good enough. Don't think I don't know it."

I'm looking at Mama, her chin in her hands, long hair streaming down her back; and suddenly I see the girl inside, looking out through aged eyes, wondering.

"It was so strange," she says, more to herself than me. "I was going to be a dancer. I mean professional. On TV. I was good, Dory. I'm not bragging. Then the next thing I knew, I had a baby in each arm and couldn't jump so high anymore . . . Don't get me wrong; God knows I love my family. I wouldn't have it any other way. But sometimes I wonder what would've happened if we didn't have to get married."

"You had to get married?"

"Did I say that?" Her hand goes to her throat.

"A second ago. You were pregnant with Bobby?"

There's a struggle in her eyes. Am I friend or foe? Too late; she has to trust me.

"I don't know what's the matter with me. I'm telling you too much."

"No you're not, Mama. I'm glad I know."

"Why?" Her fiery eyes film with tears. She challenges me.

"Because . . . because it makes you seem more like me."

"You're pregnant?"

"I mean it makes you human."

She kind of laughs. "Oh, I'm human, all right." She stabs out her cigarette. "You don't understand how it was, Dory. Nowadays, you don't have to do anything, but in those days it was different. You got pregnant, you got married. But let me tell you something: I love your father. He's a good man. I would've married him anyway. And that's the truth, and don't you ever forget it. And don't ever tell him I told you."

"I won't Mama. I love you."

"I love you too, baby. You know that, don't you?"

"I know it."

She kisses my cheek. "Come to bed."

"In a minute. I want to see how the movie ends."

How it ends is that the teenagers take over the country.

But the little kids, the preteens, resent it and revolt. That's how it ends.

[18]

Dear Bobby,

Missy's practicing (kickballchange) her tap-dancing (kickballchange). Byron and Robert are playing cards, and Mama's watching TV. Just your average American family on a typical afternoon.

Well, things are really moving along, what with Missy being on the Carson show (wasn't that something?) and now being called to do *Shoot for the Stars*. Have you seen it, Bob? It's worse than *The Gong Show*. Especially the host, Mace Mason. He'd serve up barbecued Girl Scouts if he thought it would help the ratings.

What it is, there's a panel of Grade Z celebrities. You can't remember why they're celebrated; they just do game shows. The three of them judge five different acts, and the best act wins. Except sometimes the weird-est act wins, like that man who lit his gas on fire—forget it. It's too awful.

Anyway, Robert thinks it's a good idea because lots of people watch the show. He's positive Missy will win. She's positive too. If you win, you get a bunch of cruddy prizes and a chance to compete in the finals. She says she'll win that too.

I hate the show. They laugh at you, not with you. And if they don't like your act, you don't finish. Each celebrity holds a rope attached to a cage at the back of the stage, and if one of them pulls the rope, you're Konged: a guy in a gorilla suit comes out and carries you away. Byron says it makes the Inquisition look like a Mary Kay party. So that's on Friday, and I can hardly wait. Oboyoboyoboy.

Byron took me to church the other morning. Robert let us borrow the Ford. The only True Believer church is ten miles and forty-five freeways from here, so we went to sunrise service at a drive-in church Robert told us about.

We thought it would be like the one in Elvira, where the guy stands down front and his voice comes out of the speakers. But suddenly the giant screen lights up, and the credits begin to roll.

THE CHURCH OF THE DIVINE DEDUCTION
PROUDLY PRESENTS
REV. DWAYNE STONE

[116]

The scene opens in a handsome study; even the books look polished, and a man in a yellow suit turns around and wallops us with his smile.

If Robert had a brother, this would be the guy. He was very handsome and prosperous-looking. He wanted us to be prosperous, too. He recommended joining his Ladder Club, headquartered in Reno, Nevada. For a small donation he'd send us a free book detailing his rise up the ladder of success to the top, where he's vice-president of a corporation run by Jesus. Byron held his nose and said, "The snack bar will be closing in five minutes, five minutes." It wasn't what I'd had in mind.

There are lots of strange churches out here. Also, self-help-while-u-wait places, where you pay a bunch of money and some fascist in a leisure suit tells you how messed up you are. For instance: Santa Claus Is Dead, Inc., founded by a former pinball champion; and Who The Hell Do You Think You Are?, which is a crash-course for masochists. They sit you under hot lights and tell you you're sweaty, and so forth.

A news break's on in the background, Bobby. Some people are chanting "We will not be nude!" They're artists' models at the university. They want more money, less drafts.

You know that California joke everyone likes so much at home: It takes ten Californians to change a light bulb; one to do it and nine to experience it? Well, some of that's true, but it's no crazier than Deadwood. Just different. Most of the people here are from someplace else. Robert's the only native I've met, and he's in a class by himself.

Missy says be sure to tell you to watch *Shoot for the Stars*. It's live, not prerecorded, so you'll have to check the listings. She also says to tell you nyah-nyah-nyah.

I wish you were here, Bob. Mama and Missy are so far out. I don't want to let the air out of their balloons— I just don't want them to explode. This morning Mr. Ed got jealous of a poodle the Posts adopted. Missy thinks I'm jealous of her success, but honest, Bob, I'm not. I feel as if I'm trying to protect her from something, but I don't know how or what.

Well, I better wind this up. We're going to George's Gorgette for dinner. It's one of those stuff-your-face places with huge free Pepsis with every meal. The other day I fantasized Robert going cold-turkey off Pepsi. He was screaming and climbing the walls. He says be sure to remember him to you and Daddy.

I hope your job's okay and you're not too lonesome. School starts the eighth, so we'll be home soon, I hope. Give my love to Daddy. Mama says tell him everything's fine.

> Bye, Bobby. I miss you.
> Your loving sister,
> Dory

[19]

"Mama, how can you watch those things?"

"Just leave my programs alone, Dory."

"They're so depressing."

"They're not depressing. They're true to life."

"Soap operas are true to life?"

"Dory, I'm trying to listen!"

Two women stare across a restaurant table. The twitchy blonde one speaks.

"*Well, surely you knew that—*"

"*What?*"

"*Never mind.*"

"*What were you going to say, Joyce?*"

"*I— I can't tell you, Nancy.*"

"*Why not?*"

"*He—*" *Joyce glances over both shoulders.* "*He made me promise.*"

"*Who? Joyce, you mean Robert, don't you.*"

"*I never said it was Robert!*"

"*Then why won't you look at me? Joyce, I know about Robert. Everyone knows about Robert!*"

"Who's Robert?"

"Dory, if I try to explain, I'll never catch up!"

"How can I enjoy it if I don't know who Robert is?"

"Robert," she says resentfully, "is the disco-dancing ex-husband of Larry's half-sister, Sylvia."

"So what's the big secret?"

"Dory, you're making me miss my show! It's got something to do with his past."

"What about it?"

"Larry thinks he used to be a hit man with the Mob."

"Robert was a hit man with the Mob? Are you kidding?"

"That's what Larry says! Larry's a lush."

"Mama—"

"No more questions, Dory!"

"*Why are you looking at me like that, Nancy?*"

"*I'm beginning to understand . . . You're pregnant, aren't you, Joyce.*"

"*How— how did you know?*"

"*There's just something about you—*"

"Yeah, your fat gut," Missy says, entering the room.

"Melissa Jean Woods!"

"Well, geez! These things are so stupid! Mama, I got something real important to talk to you about."

"Not now, Missy."

"It can't wait!"

"Oh, for heaven's sake!" Mama snaps off the TV. "Now what's so important it couldn't wait till the commercial?"

Missy rewards Mama with a flash of dimples and a bat of her long, mascared lashes. She's taken to wearing makeup; a touch of blush, a lick of liner. Mama hasn't said a word.

"Okay. I want my name changed. Legally. And I want everyone to call me Desiree from now on. That goes for you and Birdbrain, Doris."

"There's nothing wrong with your name—"

"I'm talking to Mama."

Mama doesn't like the legally. "I'll have to talk to Daddy, Missy."

"Desiree! Desiree!"

"Desiree," Mama sighs.

"And another thing: I want a tattoo."

"*What?*"

"Butt out, Dory."

"I don't believe this! You're nuts, you know that, Missy?"

"I want a rose. On my thigh. Kimmy has a rose—"

"Kimmy has a *baby!*" And a big old biker boyfriend. She's fourteen. She lives in the trailer court. Her ambition in life is to be a famous groupie.

"Absolutely not, Missy." Mama shakes her head.

"It's not like I want a *skull* or something! Just a rose! You should see Kimmy's!"

"Everybody sees Kimmy's," I say.

"You're just jealous 'cause she's so pretty!"

"That's a lie! I feel sorry for her."

"Oh, yeah? Well, I got news for you, Dory. She feels sorry for you!"

Only a face that beautiful can look so ugly. Missy's maimed with rage.

"Boy, are you a jerk, Missy! It's time somebody told you! You're just a spoiled little brat! Mama and Daddy treat you like a queen but—"

"Tell me about it! You wouldn't even be here except you threw such a *fit* they were afraid to not let you come! When I'm a big star—"

"Will you stop with that stuff? You're no closer to being a star than you were in Deadwood!"

"Dory!"

"Stay out of this, Mama! This is between Missy and me."

"Desiree!"

"Desiree doesn't exist, you twit!"

She bit me.

"Mama, are you just going to sit there? She bit me!"

"You were teasing her."

"Teasing her! I was telling her the truth, and you know it!"

"You wouldn't know the truth if it bit you!" Missy shrieks. "You're jealous! Jealous! That's all you are! Big, fat Dory! You make me sick!"

I leap to the sink, turn on the sprayer and let her have it, full blast.

"Quit it, Dory! You're wrecking my hair!"

"Dory, have you lost your mind?"

The door opens, and Byron and Robert walk in with a fresh supply of Pepsi.

"What in the world's going on?" Robert asks.

"Girl talk," Mama manages.

"I'll get you for this!"

"Oh, dry up, Missy."

"*Desiree!*"

Byron takes me outside to cool off.

"It's useless! Useless! Nobody listens!"

"I'm listening," he says.

"Why does she have to be such a jerk? I was telling her the truth!"

"So what do you want? A thank-you note? There's no sense getting upset."

"I give up! I just give up! And don't tell me I'm overreacting! Hysteria's the only rational response!"

The mail comes. Our hit song's returned with a letter from the publisher. He says it doesn't have a strong enough "hook" to drag people off the street and into record stores. He also says people would be embarrassed to ask for it. Who could ask for "Trash"?

This inspires Byron to sit at Robert's Remington and fire off a salvo. He says nothing embarrasses people these days, even when it should. Embarrassment, like the little toe, is on its way out. Frankly, Byron says, he's sorry to see it go. Sometimes a good blush is the only thing that keeps people honest.

[20]

I'm so nervous on the way to *Shoot for the Stars*, Robert
has to stop the car so I can throw up. This provokes
much merriment from Missy: "Geez, what a nut. You'd
think it was *her* big break," etc. She's icy calm. She
never sweats. Missy doesn't have a sweat gland in her
. body.

Then, because stardom's so close, she gets magnani-
mous and makes a speech; the gist of which is, it's perfectly normal for me to be insanely jealous of her.
Anyone would be. If she were in my shoes, impossible as
that is to imagine, she'd feel the same. I almost strangle
her.

We pull into the parking lot, horn blaring, me and
Missy screeching, and find our way to the studio where
Shoot for the Stars is shot. I mean *shot*. Once this
Konged contestant went beserk and tried to gun down
Mace Mason and the celebrity panel.

It's bedlam backstage. Someone takes Missy away
for makeup. Robert tries to butter up Mace Mason, but

Mace is in a rush. His fox terrier face is thick with orange pancake. He looks like a jack-o'-lantern.

Mama smokes two cigarettes at once. She points out the celebrity panelists: comedienne Snooky "I-was-such-an-ugly-baby-they-put-a-blanket-over-my-head-so-sleep could-creep-up-on-me" King, celebrity alcoholic Wink Dixon and actor Bo Steele, star of the late hit *Random Seven*. Once he was a child star. Now he's a professional tough guy. Mama thinks he's a hunk.

Robert says it's good luck that Missy has Wink for a panelist. But he doesn't remember her, or us, or being on the Carson show.

Missy's back, her face bright orange, rouge blooming like fever. Robert takes her aside for a last-minute pep talk. Mama checks her watch for the fifteenth time in that many minutes.

"Mama, will you please relax?"

"Relax! This could be it!"

"It's just *Shoot for the Stars*."

"Which, for your information, Doris, is watched by forty million people each week!"

"All bananas," Byron adds.

"Well, you should talk!" Mama snaps, then says, "I'm sorry, Byron. Don't take that personally."

"Wouldn't dream of it, sweetheart," Bogie says.

Robert and Missy join us, and a production assistant explains what to expect. Missy's the last act, number five, following a band named Drool, a midget comedian, a gospel singer and a juggler. She pouts until Robert convinces her they're saving best for last. She's wearing the silver-sequined outfit with red glitter stars. She's going to sing, twirl and tap "That Old Black Magic."

Suddenly Mama says: "I can't stand the suspense!"

"Get ahold of yourself, Lorraine." Robert speaks softly, but she cools right down.

"I'm sorry, Robert."

"No need to be."

He's wearing my favorite Robert outfit; the blindingly spotless white suit. I'm so glad he's here with us I almost forget that it's his fault we're here at all.

Someone hurtles down the hall screaming, "Places! Places!" Mama almost keels over. The production assistant kicks me and Byron out, and we take our seats in the front row, between two beefy young couples who look as if they'd sell their kids for tickets to this show.

A guy comes out and warms us up by telling a bunch of dirty jokes. Then the orchestra starts the *Shoot for the Stars* theme, and everyone applauds.

Mace Mason runs onstage like a delirious poodle. You'd think he was having the time of his life, though the last time I saw him he was swearing.

Wink Dixon groans when the audience applauds him. "Do you have to make so much noise?" he screams, and everyone claps again. Snooky King rips off her wig and throws it at Mace Mason. Bo Steele tells a story in hip-talk so heavy nobody understands him.

Finished with the panel, Mace says, "And now, playing their soon-to-be-a-hit song, 'We Are Insane', it's Drool!"

The curtains part, and there stand four of the most

relentlessly repulsive guys I've ever seen. They move like robots and sing like the dead: "We are in-sane, We are in-sane," over and over and over. The panel takes them seriously, awarding them 27 points out of a possible 30.

Next comes the comedian. He's not especially funny. He tells a lot of short jokes. I mean about being a midget. The audience laughs uproariously; but if he were tall, he'd be Konged for sure.

Commercial, commercial, then the gospel singer. She sings "Amazing Grace." Exquisitely. She gets 22 points; only 5 from Wink, who says Blacks should stick to dancing. Bo Steele turns to him and says, "Man, you must get nervous at Thanksgiving, cuz you're the biggest turkey I've ever seen."

Commercial, commercial, then the juggler. He's good, but a juggler nonetheless. Does he hope to one day play Carnegie Hall? Byron says no, he just wants to get on TV; but I'm not so sure.

Commercial, commercial. I slip my hand inside Byron's.

"And now, from Deadwood, Oklahoma, a little girl with a big act to grind! Missy Woods— excuse me, Desiree Jones, and 'That Old Black Magic!'"

The curtains open, and there's my baby sister, her dimples twinkling like twin stars. She salutes the audience with her baton and chirps: "I'm from Deadwood, OK., and that's Okey with me! Gentlemen, if you please?" And the band begins "That Old Black Magic."

I can't bear to watch. I cover my face. I peek between my fingers. All I can think of are those 80 million eyes focused on Missy this minute.

"That old black magic has me (thump, thump) *in its spell,*
That old black magic that you (tap, tap) *weave so well,*
Those icy fingers up and down my sp—"

Bo Steele Kongs her.

The guy in the gorilla suit gallops out of his cage, grabs Missy and runs offstage.

"Good Lord!" Byron gasps. I'm paralyzed. The audience buzzes and rumbles.

"Wait a minute," Bo says. "I got something to say. Bring back the kid."

The gorilla returns with Missy under his arm. I've never seen that expression on her face. No expression.

Bo stands and faces the audience. "I know what you guys are thinking. Right now you're saying to yourselves: 'I thought Bo Steele was a good guy. How come he Konged a kid?' Man, I don't wanna be no villain, but come on. Is this for real? Gimme a break! Listen, I did the child-star scene, and all I can say is, quel bummer, man!

"Listen, little girl, I love ya. Honey, you're a sweet kid. But let me save ya a lotta grief. Come back in a few years. Happy childhood, baby."

He sits amidst a round of applause. "This man's a real human being!" Wink sobs. The gorilla disappears with Missy. Mace screams, "Stay tuned! We'll be right back with the judges' final decision!"

I'm onstage before Byron can stop me. I grab Mace Mason's arm.

"What's going on? Since when do you Kong kids?"

"What is this? Who are you?"

"Missy's sister!"

"That's showbiz, kid. Speak to Bo."

"He's an idiot! He thought he was doing her a favor!"

"Listen, he was doing us *all* a favor."

"*You* listen, you grinning pumpkin head! I hate you, and I hate your show! That midget's going to win, and you know it! Just because he's a midget doesn't mean he's funny!"

"What's *that* supposed to mean?"

"They feel sorry for him! No one can beat him!"

"Who'd want to beat a midget?"

"*It's not funny!*"

But he escapes. I push backstage and find my mother.

She's saying, "Missy? Missy darlin', can you hear me? Darlin', why don't you say something?"

Missy's sitting on a chair, her eyes blank as mirrors. No expression. This face for rent.

Byron appears; claps his hands near her ears. She flinches.

"She can hear us," Robert says. "She's just in shock. Missy? Desiree? Speak to me, honey!"

Mama's hysterical. "What will I tell her father? Melissa Jean Woods! You stop that this minute!"

Missy gazes straight ahead, her eyes wide and empty. When Mama stops shaking her, she sags like a doll.

Robert informs Mace Mason we'll be suing him for a million. Mace quips, "Read the fine print, fool!" and hurries onstage to award the midget.

Mama says, "Dory, call your father and tell him everything's fine."

In another time zone Daddy's tearing out his hair, wondering what he'll tell all the people he told to watch the show.

"I can't, Mama! I don't know what to say!"

"Say anything! Just don't tell him the truth!"

"I can't lie good on my feet, Mama! I'm scared! What's wrong with Missy?"

"There isn't time to be scared. Your sister's going to be fine. We'll take her home, give her a nice bath, get some of that good Peach Passion—wouldn't you like that, honey?"

No reply.

"Mama—"

"Do like I say, Dory!"

She leads Missy out to the car. I find a phone.

Daddy's incoherent. He'll *kill* Bo Steele.

"I know this sounds crazy, Daddy, but it was supposed to happen that way. It's a publicity stunt. Robert arranged it. Is Bobby there?"

"Bobby's never here. Let me talk to your mother."

"I can't. She and Missy are—celebrating."

"Is Robert there?"

"He's busy, Daddy. He's talking to Mace Mason."

"Mace Mason . . ." I can see my father smile. "I can't believe this is really happening."

"Me, neither, Daddy."

"Well, I knew there was some good reason why Missy got Konged. It doesn't make much sense to me, but I suppose Robert knows what he's doing."

"You bet."

"Tell your mother to call me later. I'm too excited to sleep. And give my baby girl a big hug. Tell her I'm so proud!"

We drive back to the trailer in a silence profound as Missy's. We undress her, bathe her and put on her nightgown. Mama gives her a cup of warm milk, which she usually fights tooth and nail. She laps it up like a little cat, then climbs into bed. I turn out the light, and she closes her eyes. Gently, I kiss her forehead.

In the living room, Robert's trying to drown himself in Pepsi. Mama smokes like a fire. Byron sits on the edge of his chair, clenching and unclenching his hands.

"She'll probably be fine tomorrow," Robert says.

"Of course she'll be fine!" Mama snaps. "She's just tired!"

Her glass tips, and wine runs down her dress. "Oh, God!" she sobs, collapsing on the couch. The flab falls away from the moment, and it's Mama, clear to the bone.

"Oh, God! What are we doing here? What in God's name are we doing?"

Our eyes swing to the bedroom door, beyond which Missy lies like Sleeping Beauty.

[21]

It's late. Everyone's asleep. I'm so depressed. Blues thick as fog; I can't breathe.

Is the nightmare black or are the windows painted? I saw that scrawled in a john the other day. I've seen a lot of johns lately. My stomach's a mess.

I could wake up Byron, but Robert would wake up too, and he's the last person I want to see right now. If only I could hear Bobby's voice, that sandpaper voice rough with love . . .

Instead, I'm hearing Ray Vaughn, of Ray Vaughn Chevrolet. If I buy a new ten thousand dollar van, he'll give me two free packs of Twinkies.

"That's right, folks! We're slashing prices, smashing prices, bashing prices . . ."

This is awful. I can't stand it. I feel sure I'm going to scream. Byron says when I get depressed I should list what's wrong on paper. Corral it, not let it run wild. So here goes:

I'm plain, moody, high-strung, hairy. Scared. Of

what? Of life? *Life is a birthday present from God.* Why am I afraid to open it? What else is wrong: my sister's in Oz, my mother's in outer space. I'm so alone. Lord, what's to become of us? Where do we go from here but crazy?

I lie awake, I am like a lonely bird on the housetop. The night is bottomless, swallowing me. Bobby and I built a sandbox once, told Missy it was quicksand and threw her in. I try to be good, God. I'm so alone. Can't You find me, lost in West Hollywood?

. . . thinking about all the sadness, madness, in the world. The crying kids. How can I hope to minister, Lord, when I can't even help myself?

I'm so *scared!* What's going to happen to Missy? She's not bad; she's just a person. Just a little kid. Lord, You know how fragile we are; how easily bent in the wrong direction.

There's a talk show on now with the most awful minister. He reminds me of Reverend Roy. He can't understand why women are jumping off their pedestals and he's warning us we'll break our necks.

He says You make it plain in the Bible: Women make bread and babies and do; that we're cheerleaders in the great game of Life, and to question Your word is heresy.

But You never said that; the disciples did, and they were just people like me; trying to do good but full of fear, never understanding Your stories . . .

I life up my eyes—God, *please* bring back Missy! She's a pain and a brat, but she's ours. We love her. I know that doesn't make sense, but what does? I believe, Lord. Help my unbelief.

It's three a.m. I have to go to bed. But I'm scared to fall asleep, because then I'll have to wake up again, and Missy might still be wherever she's gone—*Oh, Lord!* Take away this fear that's strangling me! Fill me with grace and love and strength enough to meet whatever lies ahead. Thy kingdom come, Thy will be done, but *please* don't make Missy a zombie. Amen.

[22]

The doctors say there's nothing wrong with Missy.

Nothing they can fix, anyway.

Everything's in working order: her heart, her mouth, her mind. She hears, and could talk if she wanted to. She doesn't want to.

She eats, she sleeps, she watches TV. We don't know what to do. We've sung her favorite songs, told her favorite jokes, smothered her in Peach Passion. Nothing.

Mama's a wreck, plucking at her throat like there's not room enough in there to swallow. Robert keeps saying Missy's going to be fine. Over and over, like a prayer.

He's on the phone, relentlessly Robert. "Hello, my name is Robert Banks. I represent Missy Woods. Perhaps you saw her on the Carson show . . ." He doesn't mention *Shoot for the Stars*. Some of the people he's called want to meet her, but it's hard to sell a catatonic kid.

It's been three days since she checked out. It seems like three weeks. There's a vast amount of empty air time that used to be filled with her blabbing. And her singing, and her accordion, and her ever-lasting tap-dancing . . . *Due to difficulties beyond our control, we've lost the audio part of our program. No adjustment of your set is necessary* . . . The doctors say she could snap out of it anytime. Or go on this way forever.

Dear Daddy,
Don't try to find us. We've moved and changed our names . . .

We can't take her home like this. He'd flip; he'd get that way too, so that's out. She *has* to get better. And now, but how? Good old Missy, tough as a boot. Now here she is like furniture. Like a shopping cart. We just push her around.

Who would've thought I'd miss her? I'm as crazy as they say. I miss her pout, the way she hogs the bathroom, the sound of her tap shoes tattooing my brain . . .

Sometimes we have to turn to the past to illuminate the present.

Missy at two, locked in the john, laughingly filling the tub. Mama screaming: "She'll drown in there!" Daddy taking the door off the hinges, chuckling. He would've murdered me or Bobby.

Missy at four, Queen of the May, skipping through the house tossing handfuls of corn flakes. Mama following with the vacuum, humming.

Missy, through all the sun-kissed years. She wasn't prepared for this. She was prepared for stardom, for Carnegie Hall, for the whole mad world to love her.

Mama sends me and Byron out for another pound of Peach Passion. On the way back we're attacked by a pack of Gung-Hos. You can't escape them; they're everywhere.

They're followers of philosopher Gung-Ho, whose main philosophy is money. Young, mostly our age, they're obscenely clean cut, wearing crewcuts and sports jackets, even the girls. And they *smile* while they try to sell you their incense. They drive Byron nuts.

"Hi! Would you like to buy some incense?"

"No!" Byron snarls.

"Why not?"

"Because we don't want to! That's why not!"

"Why are you being so hostile?" Smile.

"Hostile! You call this hostile?"

"You're hiding something, brother. Admit it. Come clean before the Lord."

"Listen, Bozo—"

"I'll handle this, Byron. Look, I don't know your name but—"

"Carlton," the leader of the pack says. "What's yours?"

"Dory. But what we're trying to get across to you, Carlton, is that we don't want any incense and we're tired of being bugged about it all the time."

"It's only a dollar." Smile.

"I don't care if you're *giving* it away!" Byron says.

"We are. Take it. It's yours."

"No!"

"Take it! Take it! We insist!"

They insist.

"So you don't have a dollar," Carlton continues. "That's nothing to be ashamed of. Are you hungry?"

"No, we're not hungry!" Byron's foaming at the mouth.

"We're having a dinner at the temple tonight. It's free. Everyone's invited. And after dinner, Gung-Ho—"

"We're not interested, Carlton. I'm a True Believer."

"You can't be a true believer without Gung-Ho!"

"Dory," Byron hisses, "we'll miss our train. The one we're going to throw ourselves under."

Back at the trailer, we give the ice cream to Mama. It kills me to see the look in her eyes, the purple shadows beneath them.

She spoon-feeds Missy. Ice cream trickles down her chin. Weeping, Mama runs from the room. I pick up the spoon and finish feeding my sister, then Byron and I take her for a walk.

It's a gorgeous day, pastel and perfect, California showing off. An old woman at the bus stop marvels at Missy.

"My, what a pretty little thing! Isn't she a pretty little thing?"

"She's catatonic," Byron says.

The woman looks blank, then recovers brightly. "On whose side?"

We walk, Missy's hand a little bird in mine; a bird with a hopeless wing. Her pulse says life, but her eyes say no one's home. She's oblivious to the summer day, to everything.

[23]

Dear Bobby,

Please go into Missy's room and get the doll on her bed. Not the big one that talks, the little one with the squashed face, and put it in the mail right away. One of those padded bags the post office sells is fine.

Things couldn't be worse, Bob. I'll go into gory detail soon, but have to get this off right away.

Mama says be sure to send it air mail, the doll. And *whatever you do* (italics Mama's) *don't say anything to Daddy.*

I love you so much, Bobby.
Dory

[24]

"It's all set!" Robert grins hanging up the phone. "We have a two o'clock appointment with Earl Shoats!"

Mr. Shoats is an associate from Robert's past. *Which* past wasn't specified. He makes TV commercials.

Mama lets out a rebel yell and snaps into action.

"Byron, change that tie. Dory, dress your sister."

I unplug Missy from the TV, where she stares unblinking at a soap. She doesn't resist as I lead her into the bedroom and tug off her nightgown.

I dress her in the interview clothes Mama's laid out on the bed: the whipped cream dress, white anklets embroidered with flowers, and spit-polished Mary Janes.

Then I carefully comb the blond curls framing her blank baby face; the empty sky eyes, rosebud mouth, and smooth as Cool Whip cheeks.

Cool Whip. Crap. I'm eating again. Eating and eating and eating. Yesterday I ate a pie. I mean a pie. I mean the whole damn thing. Byron couldn't believe it.

Me neither. Then I ate a loaf of French bread and a box of Banana Wackies.

God, get me out of here. I'm caught in the fat trap again. Eating, then hating myself because I ate, so I flog my flab with food. Round and round like a merry-go-round spinning out of control . . .

Missy sits motionless on the bed, waiting like a windup doll. She gets fuzzy and spills; I blink away tears and lead her back into the living room.

"Well, well, well! You look so pretty, Missy! Just like a little doll!" Robert enthuses. He's pretty too, in his vanilla ice cream suit.

He polishes off his Pepsi and takes Missy's hands.

"It's going to be fine, honey. Leave it to me. Everything's under control. You just relax."

If Missy were more relaxed, she'd be dead. Mama bustles in brushing her hair.

"Dory, you're not going to wear that blouse, are you? I can see all the hair under your arms."

"Mr. Shoats isn't auditioning me, Mama."

"That's no reason to look like a hillbilly."

She follows me into the bedroom, humming; smiling at herself in the mirror. She's young again; the shadows are gone. But something makes me say:

"I hope this works out, Mama, but if it doesn't—"

"If it doesn't! What kind of attitude is that? I swear, Dory, you're such an old worry wart."

"I just hate to see you get your hopes up."

"Why shouldn't they be up? Robert says Mr. Shoats is a very important man."

"Yes, but—"

"Yes, but nothing! Not that blouse. Wear the one with the ruffle." She gives her hair a final pat, kisses me briskly and exits.

On the ride downtown Byron holds my hand. He's exchanged the palm tree tie for a palomino. It doesn't seem right, Missy not singing to the radio, but Mama and Robert eat up the silence with plans.

We glide down wide, white boulevards, up heat-soaked people-choked streets, till we reach the gleaming glass office building, sleek as the artist's conception.

We park the car in a mammoth garage, cars stacked level upon level, then take the elevator to the twenty-first floor. If Missy were talking, she'd say twenty-one's her lucky number. Robert says it instead.

"Oh, my!"

Mama gasps as the elevator opens on a hall of elegant oak doors, huge paintings and thick white carpeting. The air is rich with Muzak and Pledge. Whatever Mr. Shoats does, he must be doing it right.

We enter Suite Seven, and a beautiful receptionist smiles, her chest a gorgeous display case for a jewelers' convention of pearls.

"Hello, Robert. Long time no see. How are you?"

"Fine, Madeline. And you?"

"Just fine. I'll tell the boss you're here."

She presses a buzzer, and a voice says, "Send them in." Robert steers us inside.

The view brains me: the City of Angels captured in a wall of window. Then: the potted palms, the lush leather couches, and behind the massive desk, a massive cowboy.

We gape like hobos at a hog show: at the hat, the vest, the boots. Earl Shoats is a million guys back home rolled into one big bull.

"Rob," he drawls, rising. "How's it hanging?"

"Fine and dandy, Earl. How's yourself?"

"Can't complain."

They laugh and shake hands. I steer Missy to a chair as Robert introduces us. Mama cries gaily, "Am I mistaken, Mr. Shoats, or is that an Oklahoma accent?"

"Right as rain, ma'am. Koodegraw, precisely. Are you familiar with my neck of the woods?"

"Redneck," Byron murmurs as Mama goes on and on about her cousin Lucy from Koodegraw, who married one of the Johnson boys who made all that money in oil.

"That's known as filthy rich," Earl jokes with a wink. Mama laughs as if she's never heard it. She says how good it is to find a fellow Oklahoman, and Earl says he reckons you can take the boy out of the country, Lorraine, but you can't take the country out of the boy.

"My," Mama says when it's time to quit laughing, "what a lovely office you have, Mr. Shoats."

"It's comfortable." He shrugs. "But please, call me Earl." He lights a cigar that looks remarkably like one of his fingers; offering one to Robert, who declines, and to Byron, who accepts, much to Mama's chagrin. They busily fill the beautiful office with blue smoke.

There's something about the place that doesn't

seem quite right—besides Earl Shoats, of course. Like at any moment the *60 Minutes* crew might break down the door and start filming. If Mama knew my thoughts, she'd have my head on a plate. A curl's caught in Missy's mouth. I remove it.

"So, Rob!" Earl roars, flinging himself back in his chair. "How's it going?"

"Never been better! Did you catch us on the *Tonight* show?"

"Can't say I had the pleasure. I've been busy."

"Where's Larry? Is he still working for you?"

"That's a long story, Rob." Earl Shoats frowns. "Larry went into real estate."

"That's a nice business," Mama says.

"He means he died," Robert says. "Sorry to hear that."

"Happens to the best of us, Rob! So, Rob! What can I do for you?"

"It's what *we* can do for *you*, Earl."

Robert sets his briefcase on the desk. He gets out Missy's portfolio; hundreds of Missy pictures: Missy on horseback, Missy at the zoo, Missy pretending to be asleep, etc.

"I've got a video tape, too. You'll love it, Earl. She says the cutest things."

"She hasn't said word one since she got here," Earl points out.

"She got Konged," Mama explains quietly. "But she's coming out of it now."

"Usually you can't shut her up," Byron adds.

"That's the truth, Earl," Robert says earnestly. "This little girl's going to be big. All she needs is a break."

Earl puts his feet on his desk and puffs on his cigar. The smile crystallizes on Mama's face.

"You know I'd like to help you out, Rob. Nothing would please me more. You and me go back a long way . . . But she's too young for my movies. I'm no pervert; I don't care *what* you've heard. But Lorraine here, she might do fine. Yes, I see definite possibilities."

I don't like the way he's looking at Mama.

"What do you mean?" Robert says.

"What do you mean, what do I mean? Take off your clothes," he tells Mama.

"I beg your pardon?"

"Not here." He jerks his thumb. "In the other room."

"Robert, what's happening?"

"I'm trying to determine that, Lorraine. I get the feeling Mr. Shoats and I aren't having the same conversation."

"Don't give me that jazz! Speak English, Banks!" Earl Shoats's potato face is beet red. "You weren't trying to sell me the kid, were you? What are you, some kind of sicko?"

The moment is skidding out of control. I'm fighting to put on the brakes: EEEEEEEEEE!!!

"I think," I say, "Mr. Shoats makes blue movies."

"Blue movies! Are you from a time warp or something? This is big business, kid! Millions of bucks!"

[146]

"I don't understand." Mama tugs at her throat.

"I do." I take Missy's arm. "We're leaving."

"Dory, what's going on?"

"You know what's going on, Mama."

"Oh, I hope not!"

"What is this, Banks? What are you trying to pull?"

Mr. Shoats is still bellowing as we crowd onto the elevator, which is packed with poker-faced people. Byron holds the door, and Robert jumps in. We start down in silence. Then I explode.

"What the devil's going on, Robert?"

"Dory!" Mama hisses. "We're in an elevator!"

"I know! I'm getting that sinking feeling."

"I can explain!" Robert stammers. "It's not how it looks!"

"I hope not! It looks mighty bad!"

"The last time I saw Earl he was making used car commercials!"

"I can believe that."

"Stay out of this, Byron. I don't know *what* to believe! I just never thought you'd stoop so low, Robert."

"Dory!" Mama snaps. "I don't care what Robert's done. That's no reason to be rude."

"Rude! Mama, do you realize what just happened up there? That man was a pornographer!"

"Pornographer!" someone in the elevator gasps.

"That's got nothing to do with Robert. He was trying to help your sister."

"My sister's a vegetable! You call that help?"

[147]

"Vegetable!" someone gasps.

"Dory, I swear—" Robert's down on his knees. The elevator opens, and I grab Missy and push past him. We mill around, looking for the Ford.

"Dory—"

"*Please* don't try to explain, Robert! I'm afraid I'll start screaming if you do!"

"I know it looks awful, but you've got to believe me. *Believe* me! I didn't know! Trust me, Dory. I'm *begging* you to trust me. I'll find Missy a job!"

"You can't even find the *car*, Robert!"

"Dory," Byron says, "this is the wrong floor."

We storm upstairs. We find the Ford. No one has the keys.

"Calm down, everybody. Just calm down." Byron does his Jimmy Stewart. He's so good, we have to stop and listen. "The keys are in the ignition. Give me the briefcase, Robert."

Mama says, "Get in the car, Byron. This is no time for games."

"No game, Lorraine." He drops the Stewart. "I'm going to get Missy a job."

"Don't be ridiculous. You can't get her a job."

"Neither can her manager!"

"Doris Jane Woods! You stop that screaming!"

"I appreciate it, Byron," Robert says. "But she can't get a job if they don't see her."

"She can't get a job if they do."

"True." They shake hands. "Good luck," Robert says.

"Byron!" Mama pleads. "Listen to reason!"

He pecks my cheek, Jimmy Stewart again. "Good-bye, Doris Jane. Take care of yourself. I'll be back when I've found Miss Missy a job."

"Nice knowing you," I say. He presses my hand.

Then he's gone.

[25]

Just when things can't get worse, they do. Life's funny that way.

Byron's been gone for three days. He called last night. We couldn't make out a word he said; from the sound, he could have been at the Mardi Gras. Mama's wondering how to tell City Attorney Spears his son's at large in L.A.

The trailer—the trailer's like some avante garde art project: Funeral at the Wax Museum. Missy at the TV, Robert by the phone, waiting for a reprieve from the governor.

He came out of his room a while ago, haggard, needing a shave. He said, "I know how you feel about me, Dory, but I hope that doesn't mean we can't be friends."

I said, "I don't see why not, Robert."

He looked relieved.

Whatever Robert is—and who knows—he's *not intentionally harmful*. He can't help it, so I can't hate him. So there you have it: I *must* be crazy.

Mama's turned inside-out; all the raw seams showing. She can't eat, she can't sleep, she hasn't changed her clothes. Everytime I try to talk to her, she just starts crying.

"I know what you're thinking, Dory! It's all my fault!"

"I didn't say that, Mama."

"You don't have to. It's written all over your face!"

Missy doesn't say a word.

She's no better, no worse. She'll grow old like this: an ancient little kid. Trapped forever in a baby's body. Trapped in a baby's dream. Daddy called last night. He wanted to talk to Missy. No, Mama said, she can't talk right now; she's co-hosting the Dinah Shore show.

Outside, summer's peaking like a ripe fruit. Inside, it's the dead of winter. The trailer's a sunken submarine on the bottom of an arctic sea. No air, no light, no hope of rescue. We wait for the end, the four of us.

"Dory!" Mama lurches from the bedroom. "Get me some cigarettes."

"You have a pack."

"They're all gone."

"You smoked them?"

"No, I ate them!" she snarls, tossing me a dollar.

"I'm not buying any cigarettes, Mama."

"What did you say?" Her dull eyes blaze. Her pretty blouse is stained. Who is this woman? Where is my Mama? Where did my Mama go?

"You do like you're told, girl!"

"I won't help kill you! You'll have to do that your-self!"

"Doris Jane Woods, you do like I say, or so help me—" She raises her hand.

"I'm trying to help you, Mama, but you make it so hard!"

She sobs. She runs into the bedroom.

It's lunchtime. I feed Missy; wipe the mayonnaise off her chin. I should eat, but swallowing's too hard. I've lost five pounds since Friday.

Was it Friday that we saw Mr. Shoats? It seems like years ago. The days run together, a maze of empty daze burrowing deeply, darkly, into the future.

Robert's on the phone again. "Banks. Robert Banks. He was expecting my call . . . Did he leave a message? Well, did he say when he'll be back? He won't?"

God isn't dead; He just doesn't want to get in-volved.

Can't You find me, hopeless in Hollywood?

I believe in You, God. Do You believe in me?

The door bursts open, and it's Byron.

"Byron! Byron!" I throw my arms around him. "Where were you? I was so worried!"

"It's a long, nutty story, Dory." There's confetti in his hair, and a purple ostrich plume tucked into his hatband.

"Hi, By." Robert comes in. "How's everything in Tinsel Town?"

"Fabulous. I've got terrific news. Where's Lor-raine?"

"In the bedroom. You're not kidding, are you? Mama couldn't take it."

"Would I kid about something like this?" he says, Cagney. "Come out of there, Lorraine! We've got you surrounded."

Mama's in the doorway, migraine in her eyes. "Byron, that tie has to go."

"I got Missy a job."

It takes a minute to sink in. She clutches her throat, wildly shakes her head.

"No joke! I've got the contract right here! Mrs. Woods—a drum roll, please—your daughter is going to be the new Softwipe Girl!"

Mama swoons. "The famous toilet paper?"

"That's the one!"

Bedlam! Chaos! Congratulations! Mama smothers Byron with kisses as Robert pounds his back. I cry; I cry at the craziest times. Byron opens the briefcase and fishes out the contract.

"It's real!" Mama squeals. "I don't believe it!"

"How did you do it?" Robert humbly asks.

"They'd seen her on the Carson show, and they loved the video tape. They wanted to meet her, but I said she was too busy."

Mama grabs the contract. Her eyes bug out of her head.

"Ten thousand dollars! Byron, you're a genius!"

"Well," he says modestly, "it's only the beginning. She's starting at the bottom, but she can work her way up."

Mama flies to Missy's side. "Darlin', did you hear the good news? Byron got you a job! Baby, you're going to be the Softwipe Girl!"

Missy stares straight ahead at the TV.

"Missy! Missy, come back!" Mama sobs. "It's too late! We've lost her!"

"Hold on." Byron shoves the contract under Missy's nose. "Look, Miss. In black and white. Ten thousand clams. You're going to be the new Softwipe Girl. Missy, if you hear me, talk!"

We hold our breath, the moment frozen. Missy doesn't blink. Then—that angel face thaws, her dimples flex, her eyes come into focus and she speaks.

"Some contract! You got my name wrong, Bird-brain. It's Desiree! Desiree Jones!"

"It's a miracle!" Mama falls to her knees.

"Missy, you nitwit! Of all the ungrateful—"

"Hush, Dory." Mama's hugging Missy. "Our baby's back!"

"Quit it, Mama. Let me see that contract . . . Ten thousand bucks? Is that all?"

"I'll brain you, Missy!"

"Dory, put that shoe down!"

"But, Mama! She's worse than before!"

"Before what?" Missy says.

"What's passed is past," Mama says firmly. "Let's just forget it."

"Forget *what?*" Missy says.

Mama's on the phone to Daddy, gay as Christmas

[154]

morning. She's changed her clothes and brushed her hair and slicked her lips with gloss. No memory of the bad dreams, the dark things chasing her. Mama's in the moment, like a child.

"Ten thousand, Wey! And it's just the beginning! Oh, you're going to love California!"

Robert shaves, whistling, then opens some Pepsi and pours it all around for a toast.

"To Byron!"

"To Byron!"

"Thanks, Birdbrain," Missy says. "But Robert's my manager, so I hope you're not expecting a cut."

"Oh, I couldn't take a commission," Robert says.

"Well, of course you will!" Mama shouts from the phone. "Dory, you and Byron go get some Peach Passion. We're going to celebrate till the cows come home!"

If I open my mouth, the words will gush out like lava and bury L.A. I burn up the sidewalk to the ice cream parlor; steaming, not saying a word.

We procure the Peach Passion. We head for the trailer.

"Pretty day," Byron says. That tears it.

"What's the matter with you? Are you crazy or something? How can you be so calm?"

"But, Dory!" He's chewing his blade of grass. "Our baby's back."

"She's such a creep!"

"I thought you missed her."

"I did! That's how stupid I am! And my mother—"

[155]

"Your mother's your mother."

"Boy, that's brilliant! That really explains everything!"

"What's to explain? Why are you so mad?"

"Why am I so mad? Why am I so mad?" I ask the traffic. No one pays attention. They've seen it all before.

"There's no justice in this world, Byron! Life is a freak accident! You try and try, and what do you get?"

"Another day older and deeper in debt?"

"Why does Missy get all the breaks? She gets everything she wants!"

"For Pete's sake, Dory. It's a toilet paper commercial."

"Sure! Today the bathroom, tomorrow the world!"

"You're acting like a little kid."

"I don't care! It's not fair!"

"What's fair got to do with it? Nothing's fair."

"But that's not *fair!* Why should the Missys always win? She acts like a jerk and comes up smelling like a rose! It's not fair, Byron! It's not fair!"

I rip open the Peach Passion box and fling handfuls at a fence. The fence is graffitied: *Beam up, Scotty. There's no intelligent life on THIS planet.*

"Dory," Byron murmurs, "you're overreacting."

"Oh, yeah? Get a load of this!"

I throw down the box; I'm kicking it, stomping it, making a terrific mess. A pearl-gray Rolls Royce rolls to the curb.

"Now you've done it," Byron says. "It's the Brain Police."

A bald man sticks his head out the back window.

"You," he says to me. "What's with the ice cream?"

"It's my sister's."

"I had a brother like that." He nods. He hands me his card.

"*The* Irving Valentine, of Irving Valentine Studios?"

"There's another? What's your name, sis?"

"Dory Woods."

"Ever acted, Dory?"

"No."

"Ever wanted to?"

"Not really."

"Fabulous." His green eyes gleam. "What do you want to be when you grow up?"

"A minister."

"Fabulous. Who's he?"

"My best friend, Byron."

"Where you from, Dory?"

"Deadwood, OK., and that's Okey with me."

"Oklahoma, huh? That accent's for real?"

"You think I'd sound this way on purpose?"

"Good point."

Byron says, "What's this all about, Mr. Valentine?"

"I'm doing a new TV series. About a family. You got a family, Dory?"

"Has *she* got a family," Byron says.

"There's a big brother, little sister, parents, the works. But the middle sister's the lead, see? Think you could handle that?"

I think. "I could handle that," I say.

"Fabulous. I've got the rest of the cast; we start production next week. You'll sign the contract tomorrow. Be at the studio at ten o'clock sharp. Don't be late."

He nods to me and signals the chauffeur. The Rolls Royce rolls away. Irving Valentine sticks his head out and calls: "And Dory—don't lose any weight! You're just right!"

"Fabulous," I say.

I pick up the Peach Passion box and stuff it in a litter can.

Byron says, "Life can be a little strange."

"Amen," I say. "But it's always good for laughs."